SOLUM IRIS

Also by T.M. Ledvina

BRIMSTONE & FIRE

Of Blood, Bones, and Truth
The Phantom Flame

SOLUM IRIS

T.M. LEDVINA

*For Cathy, whose kindness was
always her greatest strength.*

*You are the little bit of light in
each of us, the softening of all
our jagged edges.*

CONTENT WARNING

Dearest reader,

While this book is a work meant to explore themes of friendship, kindness, and love, themes of loss, anxiety, and grief are present. If any of the following specific triggers make you uncomfortable, please do not read this work.

- Loss/Death of a Parent
- Bullying
- Fantasy illness

1

REVELATION

The vivid cerise blooms outside Dove Cita's house sway in the breeze. The front gate stays firmly closed, despite her wishes for it to open under the touch of the post carrier. Dove waits by the window, foot tapping an uncoordinated beat.

It doesn't matter that Prism Academy is the only university on the Azure Isles; admittance is a hard-won fight for any student granted a spot on campus. Dove has worked her whole life to be one of those lucky few. Late nights studying by candlelight, long evenings at the Nila library, and a stark loneliness born of little to no time given to social endeavors. All she can hope for now is the sacrifices she's made will be worth it.

A single, brilliant red petal falls to the ground. She follows the path it makes through the air. It skitters across the ground in a slight spring breeze off the sparkling blue ocean. The white metal gate creaks.

Dove springs off the couch and rushes to the door to meet the small, yellow-haired woman with a brown bag slung over her shoulder. Her heart is in her throat; this moment she's waited for since submitting her application paperwork months ago is finally at hand.

The post carrier reaches into her bag, producing a large envelope. Her knowing smile is soft. "For Miss Dove Cita?"

Dove can't speak—the emptiness in her stomach sucks all her breath away. She nods, taking the letter gingerly from the deliverer.

"Best of luck to you, dear," she says, her voice barely registering as Dove stares at the letter in her hands.

It is large and slightly thicker than average. Surely a good sign? When she swallows back her nerves the lump in her throat protests. It has made a home in her windpipe, waiting with as much anticipation as her. She tries clearing it to no avail.

The letter quivers. She wipes one sweat-slick palm down the length of her skirt before sliding a finger beneath the flap, savoring the last moments of unknowing. The last moments of fitful ignorance. As she pulls the letter from the envelope, her stomach is full of falling cerise blooms, a fluttery sort of sensation that is neither uncomfortable nor pleasant.

The Prism Academy logo adorns the top of the paper. A six-colored shield and a flowering laurel, with each of the color classes represented. The primaries (Red, Yellow, and Blue) comprise most of the larger flowers, while the secondaries (Orange, Green, and Violet) dot the spaces between.

She stares for a moment at the large red blooms, hope swelling in her tight chest.

Miss Cita, the letter begins, we are pleased to inform you of your acceptance to Prism Academy...

The rest of the letter blurs. The bubble in her chest bursts and covers her in a shower of relief. The sweat and shakiness are gone.

She's in. She's done it. In a few short weeks, she will be a student of Prism Academy.

Summer's end is upon the Azura Isles, and the rainy season looms. Dove smooths down the fabric of her favorite blue dress as she boards the buttercup yellow tramcar.

It's the last time she will see the streets of the isle Nila for quite some time. People dart by the tram, clad in brilliant colors. A woman dressed head to toe in red waves at someone on the other side of the street; a man with a flowing robe of blue avoids a young girl running past. Dove loves the movement of the city—will Ceruleus be the same?

The tramcar slows. Dove jumps from it, landing on the cobblestones steadily. Her destination? The port. Although she's been here a few times, this is the first she's ever traveled on the Azura Isle's ferries without her parents. She bites her lip and tightens her grip on her bag. Her head and her heart aren't in sync. She should be excited, but she instead silently begs her breakfast to stay put.

When the ferry arrives at the port in Ceruleus, Dove can't decide where to look first. The largest of the isles is an explosion of color and noise. The Blue district hosts the port—the buildings are all a stunning shade of sapphire that nearly melts into the sky. Further up the hill rests the sunset-colored Yellow district, and to the west lies the brick buildings of the Red district.

She stands on the gangway, frozen while she takes it all in, as other ferry passengers stream around her. One man bumps his shoulder into hers and murmurs an apology. She moves with the crowd then, her eyes still trained on the frenzy of color around her. She can't see the secondary districts from here, but she knows they must exist. Her own home on Nila was on the border of the Violet and Red districts. Maybe the same is true here?

Although Dove has been on Ceruleus for less than five minutes, she aches at the thought of home. She misses her mother's strong laugh, her father's quiet warmth. She shakes her head and sternly reminds herself that this is what she wants—what she has worked so hard to achieve.

Prism Academy lies in the Blue district, only a few blocks from where the ferry has docked. Luckily for Dove, the walk is close. More people her age appear from the crowded sidewalks the closer she gets to campus. She follows them up a curving, tree-lined pathway that ends at a wrought-iron gate. It stands tall into the blue sky, the oil-rubbed bronze shimmering in the midmorning's sun. Each spire is sharp, tipped with a pointed cone.

According to her acceptance letter, the Revelation Ceremony will take place in one of the largest lecture halls on campus. Dove spent several days at Nila's library searching for a detailed map of the Prism campus and firsthand accounts of the Revelation Ceremony from someone other than her mother.

Dove watches the sky. In her research, one piece of information that prevailed in all the accounts of the Revelation Ceremony was the Aura Mirror. A gift from the Goddess to the Yellow class progenitor—

Dove's thoughts screech to a halt as she runs bodily into someone. The only thing she can see is a mass of curling brown hair, but she can't stop the yelp that escapes her lips.

"Sorry!" The girl steadies Dove with hands on either shoulder. "I didn't see you!"

Dove stares. There's a fizzing low in her belly, and the warmth of the girl's hands on her shoulders is more than just simple body heat. The girl stares back, as if waiting for something. Her piercing blue eyes are framed with long lashes. A single lock of that curly hair falls between her eyes and leads Dove's gaze down the elegant slope of her nose.

She blinks; her impossibly long lashes brush against her cheeks and she smiles. "I'm Rory. Sorry again for bumping into you. Are you alright?"

Dove's tongue is too big for her mouth. But the girl, Rory, is looking at her so kindly. So Dove nods, never taking her eyes from Rory's face.

Rory's smile grows. "Okay, good." She releases Dove's shoulders, but doesn't drop her hands right away. They hover just above the ruffled sleeves of Dove's dress. Dove waits, expecting something.

Rory finally moves her hands away slowly. When Dove stays silent, she simply nods and turns away. Dove watches her meld back into the crowd of students, her disappearance sucking the warmth out of the air. As other students continue to stream around Dove, she can't shake the deep-seated feeling of finding something, only to lose it just as quickly.

Dove shakes her head. This isn't what she came here for. She worked hard to get into Prism; it isn't worth her time to worry about things that have no bearing on her education. Her goal isn't to find a mate and an appropriate job within her color class, like so many other students here. Her goal is discovery.

She follows the crowd, determination ebbing the odd feeling in her bones. She's here to learn. Learning is what she will do.

The campus is beautiful. The cerise trees with their dazzling red blooms are everywhere—several stretch long branches over the paths she must walk to reach the

Revelation Ceremony hall. One such bloom falls past her nose. She catches it, admiring its deep hue. It's the exact shade she would wish to be if her soul was Red like her mother's. Dove doesn't let the bloom go as she finally reaches the hall and follows the crowd inside.

The hall is two-tiered, the lower section filled with hundreds of wooden chairs bolted to the floor at regular intervals. More of the same chairs stand empty on a mezzanine high above. An intricate crisscrossing of beautifully carved wooden buttresses arch high over their heads to form an elegant lattice of dark wood. Massive, two-story windows on the north wall filter the warm sunlight and illuminate the space in golden light.

Dove filters in behind the crowd and takes a seat in one of the hard chairs. She shifts, finding a slightly more comfortable position before turning her focus to the front. The cerise bloom is still in her palm, resting on top of her lap as she waits.

A wiry man with gray hair and unwrinkled skin steps up onto the raised dais at the front of the room. His stride is long, his shoulders held firm as he takes a stand before the podium.

"Excuse me," he begins, his voice loud despite the chatter of students. "Students, please take a seat. We will begin the Revelation Ceremony in a few moments."

The chatter subsides as the rest of the students in the room find their way to seats. The wiry man waits patiently, his hands resting on either side of the podium. Dove plays with the cerise bloom in her lap. Images of her before the mirror at home with a red sheet are flashing through her mind at quadruple speed. What if she isn't a Red like she's dreamed? What if she is not a deep jewel tone like her parents? What if her color is washed out or faded or wrong?

Dove's hands still. Children inherit generations' worth of color traits, passed down through family members and preserved through careful mating selections. Her chances of being a Red like her mother are high. Of course, she could be a Violet, like her father, or possibly even a Blue.

She shouldn't worry, but she does anyway.

The wiry man clears his throat, and the room falls silent. "Welcome, new students, to another wonderful year at Prism Academy. I am Ash Braleburn, and I am the Deputy Chancellor. Chancellor Brigaine will be joining us momentarily. Until she does, I am here to welcome you to the school and remind you of a few ground rules."

Master Braleburn's voice is loud and scratchy, but it is easy to hear him clearly. The student beside Dove shifts, vibrating with nervous energy. Dove stays still. The roiling in her stomach argues with her decision, but she stays firm.

"First, your uniforms are mandatory. I understand the desire to express individualism, and I sympathize, however, these urges must be expressed outside of classroom hours. Accessories are allowed, including hair clips and jewelry. Second," Master Braleburn continues, his voice turning stern, "you are to sleep in your dorm room and your dorm room only. We do not tolerate late night trysts in these halls."

Mutters break out across the hall, but no objections. Master Braleburn regards the hall with clear eyes before continuing. "And last, we do not tolerate fighting or bullying on this campus. If you see any occurrence of these behaviors, please report them immediately to campus security." He stops, turning toward the side of the stage as movement flickers in the corner of Dove's eye. "And with that, I am pleased to welcome Chancellor Brigaine, and the Revelation Ceremony will begin!"

With his final declaration, two teachers wheel a massive cart across the stage, something tall and draped in a white sheet. Following behind is a tall woman dressed in a long cream skirt that swishes around her ankles as she walks. Her hair is pale yellow and curls softly around her shoulders. On her nose, she wears rounded spectacles that frame her large eyes.

She nods gracefully at Master Braleburn, and he steps aside to allow her access to the podium. She says nothing for a few moments as she waits for the teachers to finish rolling the cart to its position on the stage. Once it stops, she turns to the lecture hall and smiles.

"Welcome, new students of Prism Academy! I am Chancellor Citrinne Brigaine, and I am pleased to begin this year's Revelation Ceremony." She nods to the teachers beside the cart, and they remove the sheet.

The crowd of students titters—beneath the sheet is the Aura Mirror, the one that, through divine magic of the Goddess, reveals anyone's soul color who stands before it. It is the only mirror of its kind in all the Azure Isles. And today, every student in the lecture hall will stand before it and see their soul color for the first time.

Dove stares at the mirror with rapt attention. The cerise bloom in her palm is heavier than ever—the weight of her own expectations, her own desires manifest themselves into the delicate petals.

Chancellor Brigaine waits for the chatter to die out before speaking again. "I will ask each student to come forward when their name is called and stand before the mirror. Once your soul color is revealed, please head to the section of the lecture hall with your house color to meet your ambassador." She gestures to the back of the hall, where on the mezzanine, six students with matching uniforms in different colors wave to the crowd.

"Ambassadors will finish orientation with their houses and give a campus tour."

Dove bites her lip. She can practically taste it—her dream of roaming the stacks of the Prism Academy Library, of reading the knowledge only the books there contained about the history of the Azura Isles. Prism had knowledge she wouldn't get anywhere else.

But first, her soul. Her very essence, boiled down to a color.

The chancellor calls the first name, and the din of the room quiets, leaving behind a silence so heavy, Dove swears she can feel the weight of it on her shoulders. She can't possibly be the only one on the cusp of a dream. The silence alone tells her as much.

As the first student nears the chancellor, she gestures for them to approach her and speaks softly to them. They nod, then turn toward the unveiled mirror.

Dove has heard tales from her mother about the Aura Mirror. But now she can finally see it in action. Her hands tingle. She watches the reflection in the mirror, unblinking lest she miss the moment.

The student stares at themselves in the mirror, hands wringing in front of them. Their reflection glows, a slow start until it is as brilliant as the sun. A yellow soul, then. A kind and warm sort of person, one whose mission in life will be to serve others. What career they will choose—a doctor, a nurse, a teacher? Any of these are appropriate choices for the Yellow-souled.

Chancellor Brigaine is gesturing for the student, now a Yellow house member, to exit the stage. Their cheeks are flush as they rush to the mezzanine to meet with their house representative.

Dove watches them go with an odd sort of pressure in her chest. She shifts, then turns her gaze to the flower in her hand. The bloom is wilting under her warm grasp.

The chancellor calls forward five more students, each revealing a beautiful color in the mirror before joining their representative on the mezzanine. Dove struggles to sit still, the pressure in her chest growing with each student that finds their soul's color.

The girl she ran into on the way in, Rory, goes before Dove. When her name is called, she smiles lopsidedly and saunters down the center aisle toward the mirror.

Chancellor Brigaine speaks briefly to her, then gestures at the mirror with an elegant swoop of her hand. Rory nods and stands before the mirror.

Dove holds her breath.

Rory's reflection stays just that for several moments, no color appearing at all. Then the surrounding air darkens in the mirror, turning lavender, then indigo. But the darkening continues, the indigo going darker, and darker, and darker, until finally, the halo of color around Rory is pitch like the night.

The lecture hall is silent. No one breathes. This can't be true, can it?

Rory's soul color is Black. There hasn't been a black soul in hundreds of years. They are more extraordinary than the occasional golden soul colors that yellow lineages sometimes produce. A black soul color is an uncommon combination of each soul color, a trait that no one can figure out how to produce on purpose.

And here Rory is, with the rarest color of all.

Rory stands in front of the mirror, her mouth agape. She doesn't blink, doesn't take her eyes from her own reflection in the mirror. No one moves, not even Chancellor Brigaine. But she is the first to regain her composure. She moves to stand next to Rory in the mirror, her own yellow aura shimmering as she takes Rory by the shoulders and whispers in her ear.

Rory nods, then a professor escorts her out of the back door of the lecture hall. Dove watches her go.

Chancellor Brigaine steps back to the podium and gives the crowd an assessing look. "We are very lucky to have witnessed such a wonderful event—the appearance of a Black soul. However, students, I must ask you to continue with the Revelation Ceremony as usual." She clears her throat, then announces the next student's name.

The crowd murmurs, questions of "who was that" and "what house will she be in?" filling the lecture hall. The buzz echoes in Dove's ears, rattling around in her head as she tries to focus. When her name is finally called, she jumps in her seat.

Dove descends toward the mirror, the image of Rory with a black halo mingling with her memories of childhood in front of her own mirror. The closer she gets, the stronger the somersaults her stomach.

Chancellor Brigaine gives her a gentle smile, then leans in. "Miss Cita. When you stand in front of the mirror, it will take a few moments for it to respond to you. Just wait patiently, and your color will appear." Her words are soft, gentle, as if she can see the tumult of Dove's nerves.

She steps in front of the mirror, taking in the golden filigree on the mirror's frame that she couldn't see from her spot in the lecture hall. It curls and curves around itself, like vines that twist around drooping branches, interspersed with flowers and leaves. The single cerise bloom in her hand is bright in the reflection, but it does not match her shimmering aura.

She meets her own gaze in the mirror, waits for the shimmering to darken, for the glitter to become something. Instead it swirls, like smoke from an extinguished candle. The color is...nothing.

The titters in the audience start again, but they are not the excited ones that Rory got. Dove hears questions, so many questions that she cannot possibly answer. Why is there no color? Why is it not working?

A scream burbles in her throat, but she pushes it down, resists the urge overtaking her. She releases a shaky breath, choking on her repressed scream. Her eyes are so, so wide.

Chancellor Brigaine's golden-haloed reflection appears behind her in the mirror. "Dove," she begins, lines creasing her beautiful face, "please step away from the mirror."

"But it hasn't shown me my color yet," Dove protests. "It's not working!"

Chancellor Brigaine's expression falls, her eyebrows knitting together. "It's working, dear. You just...well, you're a special case."

Dove's face is hot, her breaths growing shallower. "What does that mean?"

"Not now, Dove. We'll explain after the ceremony is over. Please,"—she gestures to the professors standing off to the side of the dais—"follow them to my office."

Dove wants to stay, to stand stubbornly in front of the mirror until a color appears. This can't be right. There's no way this is right.

Because if it is, then Dove doesn't have a soul color.

2

———

TWIST

*P*anic. It settles between her ribs like a meal eaten too quickly. No matter how slowly she breathes, no matter how much she refuses to blink, the vision in the mirror does not change. Behind her, the chatter of the students stabs her in the back with their commentary.

"Is the mirror broken?"

"No, it couldn't be, the chancellor's color appeared fine!"

"Then what was wrong with her?"

She turns from the mirror, leaving her colorless reflection behind. The other students' musings chase her out of the lecture hall and bounce around in her skull.

They twist and turn down a series of hallways flooded with morning sun. The light is too bright against her stinging eyes—the only thing she can focus on is the sweeping gray robe of the professor in front of her. Although she's wanted to walk these halls for so many years, she can't enjoy it.

She won't cry now. If she lets go of the tenuous hold she has on her emotions, she is sure she will never regain her composure.

She's a traitor. If she really is without a soul color, then what right does she have to be here? Would this be the first and last time she'd ever see these halls ever again? Would they kick her out? How could she return to her parents in such a state?

Her stomach drops at the thought of her family. Surely, they would be disappointed in her if her soul really is colorless—if she really is the anomaly the mirror claims. She'll be shunned, have no place in their society that hinges so fully on the color of one's soul. How could any parent be proud of such a disgrace?

Although the inside of the school is warm, she shivers.

Her escort stops before a wooden door that stands at least double her height and gestures to it. She hesitates, unsure she can open the door herself, but when she pushes against the dark wood, it opens under her touch easily.

"Wait inside, please," the professor says, then promptly turns on their heel and leaves.

Dove watches them go, then turns back to the office before her, a gnawing behind her ribs.

The room is not what Dove expects. Bookshelves line three of the four walls, covering them from floor to ceiling in old tomes larger than her head. A window that overlooks the main courtyard of the school consumes the fourth wall. And in the center of the room rests a seating area with three plush chairs atop a woven rug.

In one of those chairs sits Rory, hands twisted in her lap as she stares out the window. At Dove's entrance, she springs to her feet. Her face falls when the door closes behind Dove.

"You," she breathes. It's not accusatory, or harsh, but softly surprised. "Why are you here?"

Dove just opens her mouth, then closes it again. She doesn't know what to say to Rory, how to explain why she, of all people, is in this office too. Rory is here because she is rare and beautiful and something to be celebrated.

Dove is here because she is broken.

The tears she's been holding back burst from her. She can't keep them in any longer, the pressure from restraining them for this long too much to bear. They slide down her face, the emotion filling her body to the point of spilling over. She says nothing. She can't.

There is a flurry of movement, then suddenly a pair of hands on her shoulders guiding her gently to the chairs. Dove doesn't hear what she says, only hears the gentle tone of her voice and focuses on that.

Finally, Rory's voice comes into focus. "Shh," she coos gently, "it's alright. Take your time."

"I'm—" Dove hiccups. Rory's hands cover hers in her lap. Their warm weight is grounding. Dove tries again. "I'm sorry."

Rory cocks her head. "For what?"

"You don't even know me, and you're comforting me."

The smile is unexpected; it's crooked and endearing in a way Dove can't explain. The out-of-place expression in this pit of her desperation is a shock to her system, enough so that the tears stop of their own accord. Rory squeezes her hands.

"Everyone deserves to be comforted. Even people I don't know." She bites her lip. "Or rather, *especially* people I don't know."

Dove doesn't expect the breathy laugh that escapes her, but on its sharp exhale, her tension loosens. Rory's grip on her hands is light but warm. Dove turns her palms up toward Rory's and squeezes her hands back.

"See?" Rory says, the lopsided grin back. "Feeling better already. Now tell me, uh…" She trails off, looking to Dove for something.

"Dove."

Rory nods. "*Dove.* What's got you so glum?"

"I—" Dove grits her teeth. "I'm—"

The door to the office swings open, and Chancellor Brigaine bursts into the office. She dismisses a professor and another aide with a wave of her elegant hand, then closes the door behind them with a soft and final *click.*

The chancellor makes her way to her desk and sits down in a massive wingback chair, the light from the window haloing her. It reminds Dove of the colorless sparkling halo the mirror had shown her. The thought makes her nauseous.

Rory releases Dove's hands, much to Dove's disappointment. She swears the warmth of the other girl's hands was the only thing keeping her together. But when Rory moves back to her own chair, Dove finds she can keep her composure.

Chancellor Brigaine weaves her fingers together beneath her chin, then looks over her rounded spectacles. She lets out a heavy sigh.

"Girls, I apologize." Her voice is softer than Dove expects. "This is not how I expected to begin this year."

Rory shifts. "What happened?"

The tears threaten Dove again and she swallows hard, the lump in her throat so large she fears she will stop breathing. She stares at her hands, clenched in her lap, and begs the tears to stay at bay.

"Miss Valerus, it is our sincerest pleasure that you have a black soul. This is a fortuitous occurrence, and an exceptionally rare one, even in the Academy's illustrious, long history."

"I know that. I'm asking what happened to Dove?"

At this, Dove lifts her head. The chancellor is mirroring

Rory's frown. A speck in Dove's heart flares to life, ignited by Rory's compassion.

The chancellor clears her throat, settling her laced hands on the desk before her. She says nothing for several tense heartbeats. Dove waits, Rory watches. The only sound is the ticking of a grandfather clock somewhere in the room, although Dove hadn't noticed it when she entered. It knocks against her skull, the monotonous and rhythmic ticking ratcheting her heart rate sky-high.

"She is…well, she is colorless. Solum Iris," Chancellor Brigaine finally says, sighing the last words out.

The world shatters. It's as if everything loses all color at the words, turning the world grey and lackluster. She is broken.

The cold spreads through her, starting from her neck and spreading downward. Her fingertips tingle with it, numbing them. She knows how she must look—open-mouthed, unseeing, like so many of the early ages paintings of grief. If only she could look as colorful as they do, too. But she knows now that dream is impossible.

She is colorless.

Rory stays silent, her eyes wide. The chancellor stays quiet as well, as if gauging the girls' reactions to the news. Her golden eyes swivel to Dove, watching her with a carefully neutral expression.

Rory's hand closes over hers, and Dove is crying again.

"There must be some mistake," Rory says, her voice hard. Her hand tightens over Dove's. "There's no such thing as colorless souls."

Chancellor Brigaine's smile is tight, her eyes downcast. "That's not exactly true, Rory. You know the legend of the Goddess, yes?"

Dove frowns. Every child of the Azure Isles knows the story of the Goddess Azura and her three confidants:

Aurus, Caerulum, and Lustro. The three were the progenitors of the color classes, and all the residents of the Azura Isles descended from them. But what does that have to do with her lack of a soul color?

Rory squeezes Dove's hands, pulling her from her thoughts. "Of course, but what does that have to do with Dove?"

"Possibly nothing." The chancellor shrugs. "For now, we need to keep a close eye on Dove and ensure she is safe. Colorless souls aren't normal—the Goddess' influence may have been tampered or interfered with. Or, possibly, there is something else at work here."

"Something…else?" Dove squeaks. "What do you mean?"

The chancellor shakes her head. "Nothing to concern yourself with now, Dove. We need time to investigate, and I must confer with the Aegis Order."

The Aegis Order, or the peacekeepers, record holders, researchers, and lawmakers of the Azure Isles. Their involvement in her fate means that Dove is truly exceptional, but in the worst kind of way. She'd hoped to one day work for the Aegis Order as a researcher—a dream that was surely impossible now.

Fear churns inside of Dove, a maelstrom welling in her chest. She is cold and numb all at once. The mirror, and her colorless reflection, haunt her. No matter how much she tries to shake it, to ignore the image and focus on what is happening around her, she can't.

Maybe it was a malfunction. Maybe, if she can prove she has a color, she might stay at Prism, might still hold a place in her world. She can't simply lie down and take this without exhausting every possibility.

Dove swallows. "I want to see the mirror again. Try again." Her voice is barely more than a whisper.

The chancellor's eyebrows knit together. "I suppose that would be acceptable. But Dove, the results won't change."

"Maybe the mirror was wrong."

"The mirror is never wrong."

The hot tears on her face come faster, knowing the chancellor is right. She's never heard of the mirror giving an incorrect soul color before. Dove isn't special, she isn't the exception to the rule. Instead, she is just the first anomaly.

A shout sounds from outside the door. The chancellor straightens, frowning. Her delicate glasses slide down her nose as she stands. "Excuse me, girls, I must—"

The door slams open, revealing a boy in a Prism Academy uniform, crimson jacket askew. Two professors pile in after him, scrambling for his arms. Their faces are almost as red as his jacket, their breaths coming in ragged gasps.

Rory stands, cheeks flaming red, and hands clenched in fists. "Roan!" she shrieks. "What in the Goddess' name are you doing?"

His mouth stretches into a devastating smile, then immediately drops as his gaze lands on Dove. She's sure she must look wretched—swollen eyes, tear stains, puffy cheeks. She turns her head, tracing the pattern of the rug with her eyes. Anything to avoid his gaze.

"I heard—" A scuffle comes from the doorway, and Dove peeks over her shoulder to see a professor grabbing Roan's shoulder, whipping him to face the hallway once more. "Wait! That's my sister!"

"I don't care," the professor says, pushing him back out the door forcefully. "You have interrupted the chancellor. Detention, tomorrow morning, in my office."

Roan protests, but doesn't resist the professor

pushing him back out of the open doorway. "Rory! I'm really proud of you!" His words echo in the office once the doors slam shut.

Rory sits back down, the blush that sets her cheeks alight as brilliant as a cerise bloom. She bows in her seat. "Chancellor Brigaine, I am so sorry for my brother."

The chancellor returns to her wingback chair, settling in and giving Rory a small smile. "I know Roan's antics well—don't apologize for him. He should do that himself."

Rory smiles but quickly drops it as her eyes find Dove again, still silent, face still wet. Dove doesn't feel like crying anymore. She's had enough chaos for one day.

The chancellor gently adjusts her glasses, gaze on Rory. "Since you are unique, Miss Valerus, I will allow you to choose your house. Any house is fine, but I would recommend one of the Primaries. Maybe Red, like your brother?"

Rory chews her lip. "May I have some time to consider?"

The chancellor gives her a gracious smile. "Most certainly. I'm sure Roan is still outside—why don't you go join him for a campus tour?"

"Sure." Rory stands from her chair and heads to the door. She turns back to Dove, her lips pulled tight. "Are you going to be okay?"

Dove doesn't know how to respond. She definitely isn't okay right now. Rory's presence has been a welcome buffer, but she also doesn't want to talk about her future at the Academy with someone else in the room.

She forces a small smile to her lips. "I'll be fine, Rory. Thank you."

Rory looks unconvinced, but doesn't argue as she takes her leave, bowing her head once at the chancellor. The doors open for her, and Dove hears a jovial shout before the closed door muffles the sounds.

She chews her lip, the dried tears leaving behind a salty taste.

"Dove," the chancellor says, her voice soft. "We must consult with the Aegis Order before we proceed, but I will not bar you from campus. We will make guest accommodations for you until we know how to progress."

Dove stays quiet, her hands a knotted, twisty mess in her lap. She picks at the skin around her nails, unwilling to meet the chancellor's gaze. She doesn't know how to name the fluttering in her chest. She is relieved, of course, that the chancellor is so accommodating. But her future is still so uncertain, and until the Aegis Order can deliver a ruling on her existence, she can't think of anything but that colorless reflection in the mirror.

The chancellor must understand her silence and continues.

"I understand how overwhelming this must be," she starts. "But know that I will do everything I can to protect your right to attend this school, Dove. You are a child of the Azure Isles, a child of the Goddess, and we will not deny you this opportunity I know you worked extremely hard for."

"Th-thank you, Chancellor," Dove barely manages. Her voice sounds pathetic, timid and made small thanks to the stress of the day's events.

But something like relief trickles into her veins and warms her frigid soul just a little. They haven't kicked her out—yet.

Dove exits the chancellor's office after taking a moment

to wipe her face and regain composure. She can't walk around campus with her eyes swollen, regardless of what people may think of her. They already know the worst of it—her greatest shame, her disgrace.

She does not, however, expect the welcoming party the moment she steps into the hallway. Rory is waiting, leaning against the stone wall, her arms crossed over her stomach. Roan waits too, shifting back and forth on his feet.

Rory's face is pinched, eyebrows drawn together and lips tight. She jumps up the moment Dove comes into view and quickly closes the gap between them, taking Dove's hands in her own.

"What did the chancellor say?" She squeezes her fingers around Dove's so tightly the tips turn bright red.

Dove exhales, releasing some of her pent-up tension. "She has to talk to the Aegis Order first, but I get to stay at Prism."

Rory releases her hands, then throws her arms around Dove. "Oh, thank the Goddess!"

Dove stands rigid, unsure if she should hug Rory back or not. Over Rory's shoulder, she makes eye contact with Roan. He smiles lightly, watching their exchange with an expression between pride and love. Roan winks one cerulean eye at her. A blush rises to her face. He strongly resembles Rory; his messy, dark red hair curls over his ears, and a heavy stippling of freckles dusts his nose.

Rory finally lets her go, holding Dove's shoulders like a proud mother. Dove tears her eyes from Roan and settles on Rory's piercing gaze. She's smiling broadly, that slightly crooked grin of hers that Dove can't help but grin back at.

"Come with us," Rory says, breathlessly. "Roan's going to show me around."

Dove nods, their eye contact unblinking. Roan clears his throat, making Rory drop Dove's shoulders and turn to face her brother.

His brilliant gaze lands on Dove. "We haven't been introduced," he says, extending a hand to her in an elegant gesture. "I'm Roan. Red House."

Dove hesitates before placing her hand in his. It's much bigger than hers, dwarfing her fingers as his hand closes in a tight grasp. "Dove."

"A beautiful name for an equally beautiful girl," he says, but quickly drops Dove's hand with a squawk of indignation as Rory smacks him in the shoulder.

"Do not *flirt* with my friend. *Gross.*"

Dove flushes, and she hopes the siblings don't notice, too engrossed in their playful fight. Dove watches with interest, fascinated by their dynamic. She has no siblings at home—their relationship is a new experience for her. But she can tell, even through the gentle insults and thrown elbows, that Roan and Rory must love each other.

The memory of Roan bursting into the office moments before stops her train of thought. What had he said? That he was proud of Rory? That must mean he heard about her soul color. Which means...

"So, Dove, what did the mirror reveal to you?" Roan asks, as if he can hear her thoughts.

The heat returns with vigor to Dove's cheeks. "I—it... well—"

"Goddess, Roan, why would you ask that?" Rory says.

"It's okay!" Dove holds up her hands in surrender, not wanting another argument to break out over her. "It's normal to be curious. I'm sure most of the school has heard by now, anyway." She sighs, running a finger through a lock of her hair. "I'm...well, I'm colorless. I guess."

Roan's eyebrows raise, disappearing into the curls on his forehead. "Colorless? I didn't know those even existed."

Dove shakes her head. "Neither did I. Until an hour ago, at least."

"It just means we're the rarest girls at the Academy," Rory chirps, and Dove can't help but soften at the words.

Roan seems to accept this with little question, instead flourishing his arms toward the courtyard and the buildings beyond the hallway. "Well then, rarest ladies of all, why don't you follow me on a grand tour of our glorious campus?" His eyes turn to Dove, a hint of mischief twinkling in them. He offers her a red-jacketed arm, bowing his head toward her. "I'd be honored to be your escort, miss."

The smile curves Dove lips before she is ready for it. She takes the offered arm but loops the other around Rory's. Arm in arm, they follow Roan out onto the sunny lawn.

The campus is as beautiful as she expected from a centuries-old institution like Prism. The buildings are all made from a light, sand-colored brick with delicately curving arches over windows and exterior pathways. The gilded carvings above the arches swirl and twist around each other and glint in the sun.

Dove can't believe she is finally here. After so many years spent with her nose buried in the history books of the isles, her dream of finally seeing Lustro's campus in person is unfolding before her.

She only wishes she could experience it without the impending sense of dread following in her wake.

The administration building that houses the chancellor's office is behind them, replaced by several of the academic buildings where classes are held. Across a sprawling lawn lies the dorms, and further beyond is the dining hall.

Each house has a dorm building, the sexes mixed. Roan points a long finger at one building with a red rose flag flying above the main entrance—Red's dorm. Green and Yellow flank it, while Violet, Blue, and Orange are in a row behind.

Dove stares at the flags waving in the breeze for a long time. Where will she go if she is allowed to stay at Prism? There are no dorms for the colorless, no separate building specifically for the girl with no soul color.

Rory will choose her house, since there are no houses for Black souls. They are so similar, but also so incredibly different. She harbors no hatred for Rory. After all, it isn't her fault her soul is the rarest color.

Dove jumps as a hand descends on to her shoulder. It's Roan, a soft and welcoming smile on his face. She knows she must look ridiculous, staring at the dorms like they are something completely unattainable. In a way, they are.

Roan gives her shoulder a gentle squeeze. "If you could choose, which house would you be?"

She knows he means well, but the question makes her want to cry. She doesn't know what she would pick.

She cannot choose Red house. The pain of not honoring her mother's color with her own is too sharp, too painful to bear. The only other homage to Red would be to pick Orange, but that is still a descendant, a variation of Red, and she simply can't bear the thought of trying to carry her mother's colors when she herself can't possibly do such a thing.

She cannot choose Violet, either. Knowing she failed her father just the same way as she has failed her mother leads her far away from any house that could carry her parent's colors. She can't abide by dishonoring her family that way.

And the other colors—Yellow and Blue, *feel* wrong. Dove doesn't know if this is because of what the mirror showed her. If she has gained a sense of unworthiness all because her reflection appeared no different in the Aura Mirror than any other mirror.

Every color feels unattainable, distant, an impossibility she can't hope to grasp. Even if the question is hypothetical, Dove simply cannot choose.

Rory must sense her discomfort and changes the subject before Dove can answer. "Regardless of what house Dove and I end up in, I'm looking forward to history classes!"

Dove does not miss her phrasing—*Dove and I*. As if they will be placed in the same house. As if, even though Rory is a rare, coveted soul, and Dove is nothing more than a pariah, they will somehow continue to stay like this.

"History has always been my favorite subject, too," Dove adds quietly.

Roan, apparently eager to recover from his earlier blunder, puts his nearly encyclopedic knowledge of the Prism campus on display. He urges them on, away from the dorms and toward the humanities building across the lawn. He talks about two of the history professors he knows and assures Dove they're wonderful instructors.

Despite his earlier question, Dove smiles easily at Roan's commentary. He points out interesting pieces of architecture, good places to study, and secret hideouts when you want to be alone.

Dove forgets herself during the tour—the worry, the anxiety, the stress of her newfound fate. She focuses on a future she can see. One where she, Rory, and Roan are friends. Where she studies without a care about her social standing or her position in life. A future where she isn't a rare case. Where she's just like the rest of the students at Prism.

Where she has a soul color to be proud of.

They pass other groups of students, new houses on their tours of campus. Dove tries not to notice their obvious stares, how their eyes follow her instead of their tour guide. They aren't exactly subtle in their scrutiny of her.

It's hard, but Roan and Rory keep her distracted, asking questions or turning a different direction when other students become a little too curious. Dove's chest expands each time they redirect her, heart ballooning against her ribs.

3

———

FATE

*I*t's been a few hours since Dove was last in front of Chancellor Brigaine, a few hours since she discovered her awful, terrible fate. But a few hours were enough to call in the Aegis Order, enough to create a judgement on Dove's future at Prism, and maybe for the rest of her life.

How is that fair? Her entire future reduced to a few hours. She wishes, more than anything, that she wasn't colorless.

The eyes of lingering students follow her as she makes her way back to the administrative building. Although Rory and Roan are still with her, there is only so much they can do to distract the stares. Dove breathes slowly, doing her best to ignore them.

Inside, the afternoon light sets the hallway to the chancellor's office ablaze. It's as if the hallway is painted a striking shade of orange or bathed in the pollen of spring flowers. It's lovely, but a lingering sense of foreboding turns the orange too dark, too rusted.

Dove's stomach is heavy, her shoulders are tight. Whatever comes next, she will try to handle it with grace, but her colorless soul haunts her. The memory taunts her. Over and over, it replays in her mind without ceasing.

When she arrives at the chancellor's door, a man in an imposing navy suit waits. A pair of dark, rounded glasses covers his eyes, so she cannot see his eyes. A coat, adorned with golden buttons and a variety of pins, reaches his knees.

He barely acknowledges her when she steps forward. He simply opens the door for her, gesturing curtly for her to go inside. She obeys without a glance back at the siblings waiting behind her. If these are to be her last moments at Prism, she wants to remember them with fondness. Looking back now will only tarnish that.

The door slams after she steps inside. The reverberation vibrates through her shoes, and the frisson travels up her spine.

The office hasn't changed, except for the massive Aura Mirror in the seating area and the imposing woman in a dark blue uniform standing beside it. She is tall and shapely, wearing a similar uniform to the man outside the office. Her golden adornments are more numerous than his, covering one side of her lapels completely, and nearly half of the other side. Her purple-painted lips look nearly black when she smiles at Dove.

Chancellor Brigaine is there too, seated behind her desk with her hands folded beneath her chin in a pose fit for a woman of her stature. She looks almost regal, but stress lines have creased the space between her well-manicured brows.

"Welcome, Dove. Please take a seat." The woman's voice is like honey, smooth and comforting. It plays in dissonance to her stern appearance.

Dove obeys quietly, settling her skirts around her and folding her hands gently in her lap.

"My name is Hyacinth. I'm from the Aegis Order. I'm here to discuss your results at today's Revelation Ceremony. Is that alright?"

Dove doesn't understand why she's bothering to ask—would she have a choice? Could she say no? Judging by the way the woman's eyebrows have raised, Dove suspects she already knows the answer.

"Yes, Madam Hyacinth. Is this regarding my enrollment at the academy?" Dove tries to keep her tone polite, to keep the gnawing fear out of her voice.

Hyacinth's brows lower and her face softens. "Well partially, yes. But it is also about your future."

Dove resists the urge to squirm. "Of course."

Hyacinth sighs and steps in front of the mirror, cocking a finger at Dove to join her. "We'd like to confirm your color status once more, if you wouldn't mind."

She joins Hyacinth, who is now glowing with a blue aura the color of the sky. Dove meets her own gaze in the mirror, watches the fear that flashes in her eyes.

She waits, hoping against hope that it will be different, that her aura will appear and glow and that somehow the Revelation Ceremony had all been a mistake. Maybe she will see touches of red glowing around her head. Maybe a faint trace of purple by her elbow. A soft glow of blue, like Hyacinth's, by her feet.

Today is not her lucky day. Her aura stays invisible, twinkling around her like dust motes in a ray of sunlight.

The mirror is never wrong, Chancellor Brigaine had said, hours before. She'd been right.

Hyacinth stays silent and watches Dove in the mirror with a look of vague curiosity. After several long moments, Hyacinth speaks.

"Curious," is all she says, and Dove wants to scream.

Chancellor Brigaine clears her throat, making eye

contact with Dove in the mirror. "Your enrollment at Prism is not revoked, Dove. You were admitted on your own merit, regardless of your soul color."

A phantom weight presses on Dove's upturned hands—the weight of her acceptance envelope. She tries to recreate the way her heart soared the day she received it, hoping against hope that she can summon that feeling once more.

But no matter how hard she tries, no matter how deeply she reaches for that determination that sparked her journey to Prism, no matter how hard she strains to find that flicker of purpose, she can't find it. It has disappeared, along with the last remaining shreds of hope that the mirror was wrong about her soul.

She is glad the chancellor understands the endeavors of her past, even if her soul color is an impossible hitch in her plans for her future.

"However," Hyacinth finally says, turning away from the mirror and clasping her hands behind her back, "there are some rules we must follow to keep our way of life safe."

Dove's stomach is trying to escape her body, it seems. It drops lower and lower as Hyacinth speaks, threatening to pull her heart from her body with it.

Hyacinth's face is grim as she gestures back to the chairs. "Please, get comfortable. I'm sure you have many questions."

Dove sits, crossing her legs at the ankles and once again folding her hands in her lap. She watches the chancellor out of the corner of her eye, but her gaze is on Hyacinth before her.

Hyacinth sighs. "We cannot allow you to mate, Dove." She frowns, her face a war of emotions Dove can't name. "The little we know of the colorless is…worrying, to say the least. Although you may stay enrolled, you must take precautions with how you interact with others, especially friends and other students. We do not yet understand the effects reproduction would cause from a colorless soul—we simply cannot take the risk. To you, or your future partner."

There it is. The knife in her back, the one she'd been waiting for ever since Hyacinth's dismissive *curious* moments before. But had she expected it to be this bad? Never in her wildest dreams did she consider having no soul color would leave her alone for the rest of her life.

It was too cruel a fate. Much too cruel to put on an eighteen-year-old girl who'd had her entire world shattered mere hours before, only to have the pieces ground into dust before she even had the chance to gather them. There had been no warnings, no signs. She'd started the day naively hopeful and ended it with her feet cruelly pulled from beneath her.

At least she can stay at the academy. But how much good will that do? Without a color, without a mate, she will have no place in society. What will she be able to contribute without a clan to support her? Her family line will end, the colorful lineage of her ancestors snuffed out. Because of *her.*

She is, she realizes, entirely, completely, and wholly alone. More alone than anyone on the Azure Isles has ever been before.

Hyacinth must sense her sorrow. She sits in a chair next to Dove and holds her gaze, her eyes holding compassion that wasn't there before. Dove doesn't know what she's supposed to make of the expression. Her eyes burn with repressed tears.

Dove gasps a deep breath, exhaling shakily. "What about my parents?"

Hyacinth smiles, but it has no warmth, no joy. "My partner is speaking with them right now. They will be fine, but we needed to inform them of your circumstances. After all, you will still attend Prism, yes?"

Dove nods.

Hyacinth continues. "Family day is coming up soon—you should speak with them yourself when that happens." She shifts uncomfortably in her seat. "There is one other thing you should know, Dove."

Dove's shoulders drop. What more could there possibly be? Would she die young? Sprout hair from her palms? She doesn't know if she can handle any more surprises, especially if they have been as devastating as the ones she's already gotten.

"As the colorless are unheard of, they may carry a sort of—stigma, you could say. Many people may scorn or disregard you. Some may even regard you with hatred. You must be vigilant of these kinds of behaviors, for your safety."

"You mean," Dove begins, slowly, "that people may harm me if they know I am colorless?"

Chancellor Brigaine answers before Hyacinth can. "Unfortunately, that is a possibility. Of course, the teachers and staff here at Prism Academy will do our best to ensure you are safe. But vigilance, like Hyacinth says, is of the utmost importance."

Dove doesn't know if she wants to laugh or cry. What is one more miserable thing on her plate of already miserable things? Not only is she an outcast, but now she is a pariah? Instead, she says nothing, muted by the overwhelm of thoughts in her head. Hyacinth must sense her mood as she clears her throat and stands.

"That is all the news I had to deliver. Dove, please know that if you have need of us, we are only a call away." She nods to the chancellor, and then to Dove. "Good evening."

Dove watches Hyacinth go. Her long coat flaps around her knees as she strides from the room. The door opens for her, the officer on the other side gripping the handle and bowing his head as she passes through. And when she turns around the corner, Dove glimpses Rory in the hallway, waiting.

The door closes, cutting off her view of Rory. When she disappears, an invisible string snaps inside of Dove, like the door has closed some connection she didn't know had formed. Like the physical barrier between her and Rory is leaving Dove untethered.

The rustle of cloth brings Dove's attention back to the chancellor. "Miss Cita, I know this must be a lot for you. And I understand how confused you must be. We will do everything in our power to give you as normal an education as possible. As such, I will allow you to choose your house."

At that, Dove lifts her gaze to the chancellor. "I thought—"

"I will allow you to choose your house," the chancellor repeats. "However, you must pick from the Commons, not the Primaries. Does that sound fair?"

"Yes, ma'am," Dove says, her stomach fluttering at the thought of having some sort of control over her future. It wasn't much, the simplest of things to decide, but it was better than nothing. Her powerlessness through the day had worn on her until she felt as ragged as an old flag, weathered by many years in a storm.

With a huff that was more like an exhausted exhale, the chancellor closed her eyes and leaned back in her chair. "Never in my twenty years as Chancellor have I had such a unique Revelation Ceremony. Both a colorless and a Black soul in one year? It's unheard of."

Dove squirms in her chair. "It's kind of like fate, then?"

The chancellor's amber eyes drift away, her lips pursing softly. Dove waits for her to continue, but she stays silent.

"Ma'am?"

"Fate," the chancellor muses, gaze unfocused. "Maybe." She shakes her head, then smiles up at Dove. She doesn't acknowledge the odd silence. "I'll give you until tomorrow evening to decide your house. Please return to me when you have made your choice. We have arranged guest quarters for you and Rory. I'll have a staff member show you to your room tonight."

Dove stands, a little too quickly, and bows gently to the chancellor, grateful to leave. At least tonight she can spend moe time with Rory, one of the few people who has made her feel human since her arrival at the academy. Maybe this evening will allow her to regain a sense of control and composure.

She can only hope so much before her expectations crush her.

The guest accommodation is bland, with whitewashed walls and beige beds. Although Dove knows it's temporary, the lack of color still stings.

Her list of worries only grows as the evening dims. Roan's hypothetical question from earlier is no longer hypothetical. Where will she go? What house will she choose?

"Dove?" Rory's voice is soft. She's seated on a bed, twisting the blanket between her fingers. A lock of dark brown hair has fallen over her eye.

Dove's eyes follow the twist of Rory's hair, down her hunched shoulders and to the white-knuckled grip of the blankets. Rory won't meet her eyes; they stay downcast, fixated on the cold marble tile beneath her black brogues.

"Is something wrong?" Dove asks.

Rory huffs, the lock of hair flying free and falling limply back in front of her face. "I can't believe they're letting me pick my house, but you…"

Dove thinks she understands. "We're so similar." She flops unceremoniously on the opposite bed. "But so different."

There is silence. Dove leans her head back, staring up at the ceiling and tracing invisible patterns with her eyes. If she stops for too long she'll start thinking again, and that's the last thing she wants right now.

But Rory isn't done with her. "Roan wants me to pick Red, but I don't really want to be in the same house as he is."

"Why not?"

"It feels weird," Rory says with a bit of a whine. "But I guess it's really not that weird, considering most siblings have the same soul colors."

Dove smiles. "I wouldn't know—I'm an only child."

She'd wanted a little sibling when she was a kid. Her mother had always told her she was the most perfect child they could have asked for, why would they want another? Dove used to think it was cute. But she'd grown up with only her school friends, and most of them had siblings of their own. Even now, she wished for a sibling, if only to know if she was truly a fluke for having a colorless soul. It felt selfish, wanting a blood relative just to know how much of an abnormality she really is.

Rory sighed. "Probably for the best—siblings can be so *exhausting*."

They stay silent for several moments, climbing under sheets and comforters and getting settled in beds that are not theirs. The bland sheets are scratchy and thin, starched and cleaned to perfection. They smell of nothing but soap and sunlight. When Dove buries her face into the pillow, she releases a huff of breath.

But Rory hasn't answered her question. The sheets stop rustling, and Dove turns to face the other girl before she asks again. "You're not choosing Red, then. What else does that leave?"

Rory's face is squished into the pillow. "I really don't know." She brings the comforter up to cover her face. "What... which house do you think you'll pick?"

Dove bites her lip. "I—I really can only pick Green, logically."

"Why's that?"

"Well." Dove swallows, fighting the lump in her throat. "The chancellor said I can only pick a Common."

"Then why not Orange or Violet?"

Dove knows Rory means well. That she isn't asking out of malice, but because of simple curiosity. She doesn't want to explain herself—she doesn't want to reveal the gaping wound festering in her heart. But Rory's ocean eyes stir something inside her she can't fight. As if, by explaining to Rory the parts of her she keeps hidden behind her heart, that they will become less heavy.

She has only ever confided in her mother. Friends were so brief and fleeting, never staying long enough for Dove to unlock those deeply buried doors and welcome anyone in. But Rory holds a key. She doesn't know why, but it's like she appeared haloed in light, holding a gemstone the exact shape of Dove's heart.

How does she let Rory in? This may be a start.

"My father, he's a Violet." Her words are soft. They hang in the air between their pillows, twinkling in the soft glow of the lamp on the table between them. "I—I can't choose his house."

Rory frowns, but the corners of it are soft. "You don't want to honor your parents' colors?"

She doesn't know how to respond. There is simply too much to explain, or too much that Dove herself doesn't understand either. All she can do is shake her head.

"That seems pretty unfair to yourself, you know."

"I know that," Dove agrees. "But it's too much. My mother is a Red—I can't choose Orange because of her either."

"Which leaves Green," Rory finishes.

The room is quiet once more, but this time no sheets rustle in their pause. Until she hears covers being thrown off, and soft footsteps crossing the room. Suddenly, Rory is crawling into the bed with Dove, forcing her to make room.

They lay together, face-to-face, on the too-small bed. Rory stares, a lopsided smile spreading across her lips. She shoves her hands up underneath her head, scrunching up her hair and some of the comforter for support.

Dove's heart calms, its rhythm steady and strong as Rory settles in beside her.

"If you don't mind," Rory whispers, "I think I'd like to pick Green house, too."

Dove is breathless, caught completely off guard. Rory wants to pick Green house? With her? "But why?"

Rory's one-sided grin grows. "Because that's where you're going."

"Me?"

"You."

"But I'm not—" Dove cuts herself off. She doesn't know

how to say what she's thinking—that she's not worthy of Rory. That Rory shouldn't base her whole future on her, this girl she's just met today. That Rory could pick any house, why would she pick a Common? That Rory, in all her rareness as a Black soul, would follow *her,* a colorless?

Rory turns her face up to the ceiling, eyes closed. "The thing is, Dove…I never planned for this possibility. I mean, who would? I had always just accepted that I would go where the mirror sent me. To have a choice is…unfathomable. So why would I choose to isolate myself? We're the 'rarest girls on campus,' remember?"

Heat spreads across Dove's face and prickles behind her eyes. This loyalty, this kinship, is incomprehensible. But there is a stirring inside of Dove's chest that soothes her. This is right. The two of them sticking together is the only right thing in the world, when so much of it has gone wrong.

A nudge; Rory has pushed her shoulder against Dove's. Her eyes sparkle, and that lopsided smile has returned.

"Green house it is, then?" Rory asks, holding Dove's gaze.

Dove can't help it—she returns Rory's smile, and a prickle of hope stutters to life. "Green house it is."

4

GREEN

The next morning, Dove and Rory stand side-by-side before the chancellor's door. She's already seen the intricate carvings too many times. But the heaviness that was the last day's burden is lighter; she sends a small prayer to the Goddess that she will not see these doors for a long while after this.

Her stomach is hollow as Rory knocks on the door. What if the chancellor rejects their choice of Green house? What if she splits them apart?

An invisible string connects her to Rory now. Dove senses it all the time, a sort of persistent, ever present tug deep in her belly that tethers her to the girl beside her. She doesn't know how it formed, but it is precious to her now.

But the fear still lingers, coiling its way around her chest.

"Please, come in," they hear faintly from behind the door.

Inside, the chancellor sits behind the desk, a stack of papers before her and a half-written memo sticking out of a typewriter.

"It is a welcome sight to see you again, girls." The

40

chancellor's voice is bright when she greets them.

Rory bows her head, a gesture of respect. Dove follows her lead. They sit in the plush leather chairs and wait for the chancellor to address them again. Dove's skin is prickly, like she is connected to the electricity that powers the city's streetcars.

The chancellor regards them, her eyes soft. "You are here to inform me of your house decisions?"

"We are," Rory says, glancing at Dove. Although they are choosing the same house, Rory insisted on delivering the news in tandem, positive that the chancellor would try to convince Rory otherwise. Rory wanted the chance to plead her case. "We've both decided on Green house."

Chancellor Brigaine raises her eyebrows. "Green house? Both of you? Surely, Rory, you'd want to choose a Primary?"

Rory shakes her head. "No, ma'am, I wouldn't. I want to be where Dove is."

Sensing Rory won't explain unless the chancellor presses, Dove jumps in. "We talked about it last night. It would be easier for us to be together, since we are both… unique. The transition and assimilation into Prism's culture will be easier that way."

The chancellor listens with her head slightly cocked, as if she is considering Dove's words carefully. She doesn't appear angry, but contemplative; her face is soft, with a slight curve of her lips. Dove hopes this is a good sign.

"That's an adequate reason for me. Consider yourselves a part of Green house from this day forth." She stops, flipping through the stack of paper on her desk. "Seeing as you both picked the same house, that works out serendipitously for you. You don't mind being roommates, I assume?"

Dove watches Rory's face light up, a mirror of what

her own feels like. This was more than they'd bargained for, but it was a happy accident, one that neither of them would take for granted.

"No, Chancellor, we wouldn't mind at all," Dove says, trying and failing to keep the excitement from her voice.

The chancellor smiles at them. "Then I will consider this matter resolved. Someone will bring your things to your new room for you to unpack. I suggest," she says, sliding a campus map toward them, "that you find your dorm manager when we finish here and get your keys as soon as possible." She circles a spot on the map with her pen.

Dove takes the paper with a nod. Her heart is the lightest it has been since yesterday morning. Hope swells in her chest, a tingle beneath her ribcage like that of a butterfly. Tentative, gentle, beautiful.

Rory leads the way from the chancellor's office as Dove considers that small sparkle in her chest. Hope, she thinks. Hope that, from this day on, she will have somewhere to belong.

As they walk across campus toward Green house's dorm, she glances sideways at Rory. With her by Dove's side, she suspects the hardest times are behind her. That invisible string between them braids into a cord, an unbreakable bond that grows stronger with each step they take.

Dove likes their dorm manager, Marigold. Everything about her is warm and inviting, and the moment she meets Rory and Dove, she exudes excitement. She hands them their room keys then sends them on their way with a basket full of snacks and a cheery goodbye. It's as if someone has sent her through a very sunny hurricane.

Their room is the last one on the floor, at the end of the hallway. Inside, a large, curving window takes up most of one wall of their room, giving them an excellent view of the lawn and a small thicket of trees just beyond it. Sunlight streams through, illuminating the wooden floors scuffed from years of moved furniture and dropped textbooks.

Their beds are bare, waiting for their new owners to cover them in blankets and pillows and books during the long nights of studying. They are up against a wall, side by side. A single nightstand sits between them. Two desks stay parked against the opposite wall, cream paint worn thin where elbows rested for many years.

Dove loves it instantly. It feels, even without her things, like home.

Rory must be taken with it too; her gaze lingers on the sun-dappled floors and the view out their window. The lawn is dotted with students in a variety of uniform colors. Although it's hard to see exactly what they're doing from this high up, they're fascinating to watch.

A knock interrupts her daydreams. Dove turns to answer it, but before she can, the door opens on its own.

Roan sticks his head through the gap in the door, glances between them, and finishes opening it with a bow of his head.

Rory groans. "What are you doing here, Roan?"

He grins, his teeth white and straight. "I wanted to congratulate you and Dove on selecting your house."

Heat rises in her cheeks. His appearance is unexpected; that alone is enough to make her stomach queasy. But it doesn't help that, even without her things, Roan's appearance in their room feels like an admission of sorts. A glimpse into her most private space. And it's *mortifying*.

Rory crosses her arms over her chest with a huff, then sits on an elegant chair by the desks. "You mean, you're here to grill me on why I didn't choose Red house?"

Roan's grin fades a bit, but he recovers quickly. "No, I'm not. I think it's great you chose a house that satisfies you." He sighs and leans against the doorframe. "I just want you to be happy, okay?"

His eyes flick over to Dove, and his face softens. She says nothing, unsure what the look means. Roan seems confused when he looks at her, like he doesn't quite know what to make of her—like he doesn't understand her. She shakes her head, sure she's overthinking.

"And Dove," he says, his smile returning, "I'm glad you're here for Rory."

A giggle escapes on a soft huff of breath; she clears her throat to cover it, but knows she has failed when Roan's smile gets wider.

"Rory and I are in this together." Dove lifts her chin, ignoring the way her cheeks are burning even hotter now. "That's why we picked the same house. The rarest girls on campus, remember?"

"That's right." Rory appears at her side, lips set in a resolute line.

"It's just nice to see you happy." Roan holds up his hands in surrender.

Dove softens. Rory shakes her head, then crosses the room to take Roan in a hug. He wastes no time wrapping his arms around her and resting his cheek on her head.

Before their hug ends, another knock sounds from the door. This time, when Dove opens it, a staff member is there with a massive cart full of their boxes.

Roan helps them unload, sorting Dove's things from

Rory's and placing them on their chosen beds—Rory closer to the door, Dove closer to the window. When their things are unloaded, the staff member leaves with a small nod of their head. Dove thanks them, and turns back to the room, hands on her hips.

Rory turns to her brother, making a shooing gesture with her hands. "Roan, it's girl time. We've got to unpack, so please leave."

Roan laughs. "I get it. Have fun!"

He saunters to the door and closes it behind him without a glance back. Dove waits until the door is shut before she pulls the nearest box to her and opens it.

Inside is a small dove-shaped pillow nested on top of other bedding and blankets. It's a toy her mother got for her when she was young, after she'd asked about the origin of her name. Knowing they named her after a bird had initially been embarrassing until her mother explained what a dove symbolized: harmony, peace, freedom, and love. She thought maybe it was a pretty wonderful thing to be named after that.

The toy had been a sort of peace offering, and since then, Dove loved her namesake. But it was a toy, nonetheless, and she didn't want Roan seeing it. Rory, however, would probably find it cute.

She takes it out of the box and places it on the bed. Rory is doing much of the same, silently pulling sheets and haphazardly packed clothing from her boxes.

They dance around each other for the better half of an hour, organizing and reorganizing their things in the space as best as they could fit them. Before long, the room transforms from nice to homey. If Dove had loved the room before, she loves it even more now.

Her favorite and most treasured books sit on the desk, stacked up three high in several piles. The dove plush is in the middle of a mound of pillows covered in lilac bedsheets and a cream comforter with frills.

Rory's side of the room differs vastly from her own; a multicolor gingham comforter drapes haphazardly over the bed, and several unfolded sweaters await Rory's attention atop her pillows. Nothing matches, and nothing is neat.

Dove likes the chaos; it's exactly what she expects from Rory.

Rory continues to flit about, never finishing a single task before noticing something else that requires her attention. Before long, a semblance of order takes shape. It's as if Dove can see the thought process in Rory's mess.

But before Rory finishes any of the tasks she began, she turns to Dove. "What do you say to a bit of fun before classes start?"

Dove cocks her head, intrigued. "What do you have in mind?"

Rory's crooked grin is back. "You'll see. Do you trust me?"

Dove ponders the question for a moment. After all Rory has done for her, after all she has given up to stay with Dove, of course she trusts Rory. She knows it's probably an innocent question, or a rhetorical one.

She nods, and Rory's grin grows. "Let's go!"

Dove lets herself be pulled out the door and into the morning sun.

Rory won't tell her where they are heading, just tugs insistently at Dove's sleeve. Dove doesn't mind.

They fly through campus, the bewildered looks of other students only registering briefly in Dove's mind. All that's there is Rory, laughing, holding her hand, backdropped by vivid green all around.

Rory leads her through a narrow passage between two buildings, their shoulders scraping along the stone. Dove holds her breath as they pass, but when they burst out the other side, she finds herself unable to contain her laughter. It tumbles from her, pure and joyous.

They pass beneath a willow tree, its branches hanging low enough to pool on the grass like water. It parts like curtains for them as they weave through the leaves. Next they pass by a small wooden cart, piled high with cerise blooms and lilacs and a variety of other flowers in every color Dove can imagine.

The ground beneath her feet turns soft, the shifting beneath her shoes making it hard to keep the pace they'd been going this whole time. They've made it to the beach.

Rory finally skids to a halt, her breaths coming in small gasps as she stares out over the vibrant cerulean ocean. The waves are calm today as they gently lap near their feet.

"I know this sounds stupid, coming from any of us island kids," Rory says, eyes fixed on the sunlit water, "but I've always thought the ocean is the prettiest sight to see in the Azure Isles."

Dove stares at the vast expanse of blue before her and can't help but agree. "It's not stupid," she says softly, barely louder than the swoosh of waves.

Rory hasn't let go of her hand, either. She squeezes tight, but her eyes remain on the water. "I wanted to come here one more time before I started at Prism. I'm…glad I could bring you, too."

"I'm glad you brought me." Dove squeezes back.

They stand there, staring out at the waves, for several long minutes before Rory releases her hand and walks up the beach, scanning the waves. Dove doesn't know what they're looking for, but she follows, keeping her eyes on the beach.

Before long, Rory exclaims, crouching down to grab something from a quickly retreating wave. Dove scrambles over as Rory holds it to the sun.

It's a piece of glass, edges worn smooth from years of tumbling in the water. It is nearly translucent, crystalline as the clearest spring water. The sun reflecting through it casts a shadow on Rory's face that resembles the crescent moon.

She holds it out to Dove. "It's kind of like you," she says softly. "It has no color, and yet…"

Dove takes the glass, holding it in her palm and trying not to cry. She knows what Rory is saying. It has no color, yet it is such a beautiful thing. A small piece of treasure that, although it has no value, can bring such joy.

She rubs her finger over the glass. It's a marvel, how smooth the ocean can make something like glass. The gentlest of movements can dull something with such sharp and dangerous edges.

Dove closes her fist around the sea glass and pockets it. It's her first gift from Rory, and she will treasure it.

Their beach trip doesn't end with the first piece of glass—they search for more, scanning the waves as they wash up and ebb back. They pick up rocks and seashells and marvel at interesting bits of wood. They kick off their shoes and run into the shallows, kicking up water and giggling until they collapse again on the beach, letting the sun dry their feet.

And when the sun starts its descent toward the horizon, Dove reluctantly puts her shoes back on, pocketing the rest of her treasures with Rory's sea glass.

5

———

ROAN

*D*ove tugs at her skirt in the mirror, adjusting it again for what feels like the hundredth time in the last ten minutes. It's plaid, green and cream, and reaches just to the tops of her knees. A cream neck bow sits just above a matching blazer.

It's a cute uniform, overall. She's not offended by the style, and it's rather comfortable. But she scuffs the heels of her black loafers on the floor anyway, rubbing the marks they leave behind with the toe of her shoe. She repeats this action over and over, stuck in a loop.

Dove doesn't know what the students will say, what they will think. Will they be angry with her? Will they hate her for trying to fit in?

The chancellor and Hyacinth's warning has been on repeat since she donned the skirt this morning—*you need to be vigilant.* She's terrified of what the other students might think, and putting on the uniform only makes it feel like she's instigating their wrath. But it might be worse if she *doesn't* wear the uniform.

She's got no choice.

Rory appears behind her. She's wearing a similar

49

version to Dove's uniform, but instead of a pleated skirt, she wears a pair of plaid pants. Her crooked smile is bright, missing any of the tension that radiates through Dove. "You look incredible, Dove! Don't worry, you're going to be fine."

Dove tries to give Rory a smile, but it comes out watery and half-hearted. "I'm nervous what others will say."

"Who cares," Rory scoffs. "They can talk, but they don't know *you*." Rory pats her on the shoulder before turning away.

Dove scuffs the floor again with her shoe. If only she could have Rory's confidence, her surety. Then maybe she could face this day, full of unknowns, with her head high. But she can't focus—she can't think.

Rory is right. They don't know the real her. And that's the problem.

She turns from the mirror, searching for her backpack and her class schedule. Her first class is language arts, and then she has a break before heading to history. She stares at the class titles, biting her lip. Maybe she'll learn more about the colorless, why she is such an anomaly. Now, more than ever, she needs to understand as much as she can about the islands, what happened to the Goddess who breathed color into them, and why she has not been graced with the Goddess' gift.

Dove is walking on pins and needles as they exit the Green dorm. Students openly stare at her, although none approach.

The girls part ways only a few minutes into their walk—Rory is off to the science building while Dove heads for humanities. She tries to ignore the stares, more prominent now that she is alone. No one approaches her as she keeps her head down and heads across campus.

Rumors of her colorlessness must have spread quickly. Although everyone leaves her be, the burn of their stares makes her itch. She keeps her gaze on the ground, only lifting her eyes enough to see where she's going.

Optimism settles in as she makes her way toward the humanities building. Every uninterrupted step she takes is a victory she wasn't sure she would claim. So when she nearly runs headlong into a boy who steps into her path, arms crossed over his chest, her heart thuds uncomfortably against her ribcage. He's wearing the uniform of the Blue house, checkered navy pants and all. He's tall with hair like a deer's hide. The sneer on his face mars any beauty he might have possessed.

"Where do you think you're going, colorless?" His voice is like daggers, sharp and mocking and nasally.

"Excuse me," she says, moving around him, but he steps in her way. She tries twice, each time to no avail. He blocks her way like a boulder and seems disinclined to move at all. She can't be late on her first day.

The boy laughs, a taunting sort of noise. "Oh ho, the colorless thinks she's funny. Well, I'm not laughing."

Dove resists the urge to point out that he is indeed laughing, but it might not be the best course of action to anger this boy any further.

"I'm just trying to get to class," she says softly, keeping her tone even. "Would you please move so I may do so?"

The boy makes a show of thinking, but Dove already knows where this is going. "Hmm, no, I don't think I will. You don't deserve to be here."

Dove's worst fears take form as the boy uncrosses his arms and reaches for her. She doesn't know what to do, if she should flee or try to fight back or scream for help. She's probably fast enough to get away from him, but as she turns to do exactly that, another boy is standing with his arms crossed behind her, and another to either side. She's surrounded.

Panic fills her veins as the boys get closer. Her fingers ache in her clenched fists. She won't be able to defend herself—the boys are all much bigger and much stronger than she is. Screaming won't do much either, although it might alert a staff member to her situation.

In a split second decision, Dove takes a deep breath and opens her mouth to scream. It comes out as a strangled cry instead as she's pulled backward by her blazer.

"Need help?" A voice she recognizes rumbles from behind her, and when she turns to look, there is a crooked smile and a flash of red. Roan.

"Please," she says weakly. "I didn't do anything."

He nods. "I know. They're just bullies. I thought we'd be past this sort of thing at Prism, but I guess the world doesn't like change." He steps in front of her, head held high. "Seriously? Picking on someone for something she can't help? That's low."

Dove clasps her hands over her chest. She doesn't like the idea of Roan fighting, especially not for her. "I should get someone, shouldn't I?"

He shakes his head. "Don't worry about it. Just get out of here. I'll take care of them."

"But—"

"Just go!" He cries, pointing. "I'm known for being a troublemaker, you don't need to get caught up in this."

She hesitates, but after a furious, pointed look, she's scrambling away as fast as she can go. The boy who'd stopped her watches as she runs, but Roan says something to draw his attention away.

Tears sting the corners of her eyes, but she refuses to cry. She is such an idiot—if she'd been paying closer attention, if she'd been *vigilant*, she could have avoided this altogether. She wouldn't have needed to get Roan involved. She wouldn't have put him in danger.

She grabs the closest staff member as soon as she enters the humanities building and tells them what is happening in the courtyard. They nod and scurry away.

Glancing at the clock, she groans. She's late.

Her language arts professor, thankfully, is the understanding type. After a brief, harried explanation of her situation, the professor simply waves her into a seat.

The class proceeds without incident, and soon Dove forgets all about the boys and the harassment she faced. The professor is knowledgeable and interesting, his lecture engaging enough that when he declares their time over, she doesn't want to leave.

But she has a break, and she knows exactly where she wants to go.

She packs her bags and thanks the professor once more before heading out the door and down the marble staircase toward the row of doors. The building is four floors, the marble zig-zagging staircase the main feature of the interior. The carved newel posts on the first floor are shaped like phoenixes, wings spread wide.

When Dove steps outside, the memory of the harassment comes back in full force. She grips the strap of her bag tightly before heading down the front stairs slowly, taking each step timidly.

The boys are gone—that is expected. But the memory

remains: the vivid one of Roan tugging her backward, of his crooked smile. How he'd taken them on without a second thought for his own safety. How he'd told her to go.

As if by magic, Roan is there. Leaning against the stone of the base of the stairs, hands tucked into the pockets of his red plaid pants.

He spots her and smiles brilliantly. "Just the girl I wanted to see. How was your first class?"

She doesn't know what to say. How is he here already? She hadn't taken that long to leave class, and there was no way he'd been on time for his own. Had he just…skipped entirely?

Dove can't put the thoughts racing through her head into words, so all that comes out of her mouth at first is a croak. Cheeks burning, she tries again. "It was fine. But why are you here, Roan? Didn't you have class?"

Roan raises his eyebrows at her. "Sure did—in this building." He points behind her, looking up at her through his lashes.

Of *course*. She's so stupid. Why else would he have been on this side of campus, been so close when the boys had troubled her? It wasn't like he was following her around, making sure no one did her any harm. That would be ridiculous.

Dove tries to ignore her burning face. "That makes sense." She toys with her hair, twisting a lock around her finger as she musters the courage to continue. "I—I should thank you. For what you did earlier."

Roan gestures for her to come down the steps. She obeys, slowly.

"You didn't deserve what they said to you back there," he says when she meets him at the base of the stairs. "I did what any sane person would do and defended you."

She looks at her feet. "Still, you didn't have to. Thank you."

Roan laughs. It's as pure as a piece of sea glass. "I'm glad to help you anytime, Dove."

They walk side by side. She watches him from the corner of her eye, noting the color in his cheeks and how his eyes match the sky.

He meets her gaze with a sidelong glance of his own. "Where to?"

Dove smiles. "I was going to head down to the beach for my break. Want to join me?"

Roan's smile is lopsided this time, reminding her so much of Rory's signature grin that she nearly stops dead in her tracks. "I'd love to."

Their journey to the beach is much less frantic than her adventure with Rory yesterday, They walk casually, strolling through the campus trails and alleyways without pressure or urgency. She has time, and she's enjoying Roan's company. There is no need to rush.

When the beach appears before her after a bend in the path, Roan steps out in front of her and gestures toward the ocean like they are about to enter a grand ball. He's slightly bowed at the waist, his deep sapphire eyes locked on hers.

"After you," he says, the picture of gallantry.

She smiles and steps down lightly. He keeps his gentlemanly demeanor as they continue across the sand, then bows by a bench just before the boardwalk. She sits at his insistence, and he joins her a moment later.

"What was that?" Dove asks, her gaze on his profile. His jaw is sharp, elegant, like he was carved from marble.

He doesn't turn to look at her—his gaze lingers on the ocean. But there's a hint of a smile creeping onto his lips as he replies, "I thought you might need a reminder that you're worthy of being treated kindly."

Dove's heart flutters. It's the most thoughtful thing someone has done for her in a very long time, even if the gesture was small.

She gazes at Roan quietly from the corner of her eye, taking in everything she can see. Merging it with all the things that she *can't* see: how kind and caring he is, how he can be goofy, how he thinks of others before himself. She hasn't even known him for two days, but Roan has already proven himself to be one of the kindest people she's ever met.

Dove doesn't know what she's done to deserve such attention from him.

Her throat is tight as she replies, finally. "You're incredibly kind, Roan."

He laughs, and she watches the bob of his throat as he does. The pause after is too long, as if he doesn't know how to respond to her statement. His gaze rests on the ocean, face neutral.

"No, I'm not."

She wants to argue. She wants to tell him he's wrong, that he should be kinder to himself, that he should see all the good in himself that she sees in him. But as she stares at his blank expression, she knows he must have heard it before.

"Even if you don't believe it, I do." Her voice is small, timid, as she whispers the words to him.

They sit in silence for a long time, the breeze warm on her skin and in her hair as it ruffles her locks out of place. The ocean is calm today, the waves on the shore gentle as they reach up, up, up, and fall back again.

The sun is nearing its zenith, glittering against the blue of the ocean. Each wave sends the rays reflecting off the water scattering frantically, dancing a frenetic piece she can't help but follow, enraptured.

"My parents and I used to walk along this beach all the time," Roan says into the space between. "And when Rory came along, she used to play in the waves. It was our favorite place to come as a family."

Dove turns to face Roan, expecting to see him smiling at the memory. What she got instead was pain. His lips are pulled tight, thin and white with stress. She is afraid to ask, but feels like she must.

"What happened?" The words are barely more than a whisper.

Roan's frown deepens. "My mother got sick right after my eighteenth birthday, right after I came to Prism. We still don't know what happened. But eventually, she got so bad she couldn't even walk anymore. All her color faded—she was like…a ghost."

It sounds awful to Dove. To lose your mother like that would be agonizing to watch.

"I didn't want to go," Roan continues, "to Prism, I mean. But she would have wanted me to."

"Roan, I—" Her throat constricts and cuts off whatever else she is going to say, whatever else is stirring in her heart.

Watching someone you love fade like that…Dove can't imagine how that feels. How hard that must have been on Roan and Rory. How hard it must have been for Roan to leave her, how difficult it was to accept that he wouldn't ever see his mother the way he remembered her.

Her thoughts stop short at Rory—how she never would have known either of the siblings had been through something so heartbreaking and painful. It is an awful thing to be so good at concealing pain—it means they have practice. That alone breaks her heart all over again.

Roan shakes his head and stands. "The past is the

past, Dove, and we're doing our best to live our lives the way she would have wanted us to." He smiles and gestures toward the stairs. "Come on. Break time's just about over."

She doesn't return his smile, but she stands and follows him anyway, letting the beach fade into memory behind her.

6

DRAIN

Dove's first day concludes with a trip to the dining hall. Although she doesn't mind spending time alone, she can't help but notice how every table is occupied with multiple people, laughing and talking jovially. Her presence seems to dull the conversations, the students' focuses trailing after her.

She grabs a tray and a bowl and gathers her meal with as much patience as she can spare, but she's ravenous. The woman serving soup gives her extra, laughing as Dove thanks her profusely.

Her destination is an empty section of seats at the end of one of the long dark tables. She places her tray down with a small clatter, but another, louder commotion echoes from somewhere behind her. Dove turns to face the disturbance, and her gaze lands on a group of people kneeling on the ground.

Someone has collapsed.

Dove doesn't know why, but she abandons her dinner and runs toward the person on the ground. As she gets closer, she can see navy checkered pants and brown shoes. Several of the boys kneeling are wearing Blue house colors as well.

One of them turns toward her, and she stops in her tracks. She recognizes him—he was there that morning, outside the language arts building.

His lips pull up in a nasty sneer, and he lifts a finger to point at her. "It's her fault! The colorless girl did this to Lapis!"

She can't help but look at the boy on the ground again. Where soft brown hair used to be, there were instead streaks of gray. The boy who'd tried to hurt her...

He was losing his color.

Dove backs away from the boy on the ground. It's not her fault—how could it be? What could she possibly have done to him?

But no one else knows that. All eyes in the dining hall turn toward her. Whispers creep up around her, and several students sitting near her scramble away, snatching bags and trays and friends in their hurry to move away from her.

She has to stand up for herself. But she can't find the words to do so. Everything she could say gets stuck in her throat—it wasn't her fault, she doesn't even know what is wrong with the boy, that obviously they are using her as a scapegoat. A roaring takes over her hearing; tingles travel up her spine. She's like a book that's been tossed from a library shelf, pages torn and crumpled on the floor.

"Back off!" Someone says.

Rory appears beside her, hands on her hips and brows furrowed. Relief floods her veins, but it doesn't last long.

"Did you hear me?" Rory continues, staring at the boy who accused Dove. "Instead of pointing fingers, try taking him to medical."

The boy turns his sneer on Rory. Her advice is already being followed, as several of the Blue house boys are lifting their unconscious friend from the ground, supporting him under his arms and legs. But the boy never takes his eyes from Dove and Rory, his face never softens into anything other than a grimace.

As they carry the unconscious boy to the entrance, the group shoves past Dove. They knock her with their elbows, catching her with their knees, and whisper horrible things to her as they pass by.

"You'd better prepare yourself, colorless scum."

"I hope you shrivel and die."

"Disgusting, colorless trash."

Rory scowls at each of them, pushing their elbows away from Dove and kicking back at them when they try to lash out. There is nothing Rory can do to stop the comments, though. Instead, she laughs at each one, calling them pathetic, weasel-nosed losers or commenting on the state of their hair.

When they finally leave, the dining hall is in complete silence.

Dove hangs her head. Even though she's done nothing wrong, she can't stand the focus on her. The students that, before this, have only looked at her with mild curiosity or confusion. They now look at her with fear and apprehension.

"Come on Dove," Rory says, grabbing her hand and tugging her back to the food stations. "Let's get dinner to go."

They do exactly that, abandoning Dove's original meal for a takeout container of soup and sandwiches the woman hands Rory with shaking hands. Dove can't meet her eyes either. Her gaze stays on the ground as Rory leads her back to their dorm. The brick and cobblestone pathways are monotonous, but Dove's stomach roils. She closes her eyes and lets Rory lead her, focusing entirely on keeping the meager contents of her stomach in their place.

When the door to their dorm room finally closes behind her, she can no longer hold herself up. Her muscles are liquid, as if she's run a marathon with no training. She drags herself to her bed and flops onto it, heavily. Rory sets their food on the desk before joining her.

She says nothing, instead wrapping Dove in a hug and leaning her head into the crook of Dove's neck. Dove stays still, staring at the floor, allowing herself to get lost in Rory's arms.

Their room blurs, and the tears on her face carve hot lines down her cheeks.

Rory lifts her head and turns Dove to face her, gently lowering Dove's head to her shoulder. "Cry on me, Dove."

Dove does. She holds nothing back, her wails loud but muffled by Rory's soft cotton sweater. She doesn't hold Rory back. Her hands stay limp in her own lap as she lets everything go, lets herself fall apart in Rory's arms.

"Goddess, you don't deserve any of this," Rory whispers, stroking Dove's hair the way her mother does. "You did nothing wrong."

It doesn't matter. It doesn't matter that she's done nothing. What matters is that she is other, she is something that everyone else is not, and she is something no one understands. Rory can't possibly fathom that—her soul is all the colors. Hers is none.

She is alone, she is hated, and everyone will condemn her for something she can't even control. How is it fair that she should have to live through this? How is it fair that everyone gets to blame her without taking the chance to hear her side?

Her fate was decided the moment her soul never appeared in the mirror. Her fate was sealed the minute that boy pointed his finger at her and accused her of hurting his friend.

Every bit of frustration, anger, and pain was shrieking out of her, tearing her throat to shreds as she screamed into Rory's shoulder. She'd never cried like this in her life. This chest-splitting pain was one she'd never felt before. It *hurt*. It was visceral and raw and more painful than anything she'd ever experienced.

She doesn't know when she falls asleep—she just knows that her body is so weak she can't hold herself up anymore. Her head falls gently onto her pillows and sheets are pulled up around her shoulders.

And before she lets the blackness take her, there is a soft press of lips on her forehead.

She's woken from her restless slumber the next morning by a knock at the door.

Rory is already awake and moving, if the soft shuffling is any indication. Dove pries her eyes open, glued shut from a night of crying and falling asleep with wet eyes. She simply lays in bed while Rory talks to whoever is at their door. She can't hear well enough to determine who it might be, and she's uninterested in speculating.

Their talk lasts no longer than a minute, and then Rory is closing the door gently again. Dove's eyes are open, staring at their cream-colored ceiling, but seeing nothing.

The bed shifts. Rory gently strokes her hair. "Dove?" Her voice is so quiet, Dove can barely hear her.

She turns her head, only a little, to face Rory. She

knows she must look awful. Her face is swollen, hot, and dirty from all the tears. But Rory doesn't seem phased. She smiles when their eyes meet.

"Do you need to sleep more?" she asks gently.

Dove shakes her head. She can't possibly—even though she slept so awfully the night before, any more will make her heavier than she already is.

Rory nods. "Okay. Do you want to get up? I can grab you some breakfast, or maybe tea?"

Dove stares at her for a moment, then down to the blankets, then back to Rory's face. She doesn't know what to say. She doesn't know what to do, either. Should she get up and walk through campus like nothing is wrong? Ignore the inevitable rumors that will have spread about her? Pretend like she can't hear them?

She knows the answer, but it still paralyzes her. She *should* get up. She *should* ignore whatever inevitability is heading her way. But she *can't*.

"You can stay here," Rory offers. "I'll get you something."

"Y—" Dove tries, but her voice is gone. Instead, it comes out as a croak.

Rory pats her arm. "I'll get you water, hold on."

Rory busies herself for a minute, grabbing a glass from a small cupboard and leaving the room briefly. When she returns, she sets the filled glass on the table between their beds.

"Here. Whenever you're ready."

Dove sits up slowly, her stomach muscles screaming in protest. Who knew that screaming your heart out led to this? She rubs the sleep from her eyes, the grit rolling away. She needs to wash her face badly. But that can come later.

She drinks the water, sipping it at first, then gulping it

when her mouth and throat scream for more. She finishes it faster than she expected and thunks the glass back onto the table.

"Rory," Dove tries again, and is satisfied to find her voice is at least clear. "You don't have to do all this for me."

Rory gives her a soft, crooked smile. "You're right, I don't have to. But I want to."

Dove's heart is in her throat. What did she ever do to deserve someone like Rory? They'd become friends quickly, sure, but to deserve such loyalty from her? Dove didn't know what could have led Rory to such a conclusion about her—that she was so worthy of this unwavering kindness was unfathomable to Dove.

But her traitorous stomach answers Dove's dilemma, loudly. She didn't eat last night, even after she'd been ravenous, so naturally, she is starving. Although her brain doesn't particularly want anything, her stomach is in stark disagreement.

Rory laughs softly. "Stay here, Dove. I'll get you something to eat."

Dove bites her lip, but doesn't protest. Rory is out the door in a flash, pulling a cream-colored umbrella from her closet before she does. Dove glances out their window and understands.

Outside, it's pouring.

Fat drops splatter on the light paver stones of the walkways, on the windows, and on the rooftops. They aren't heavy, but she can see the dark clouds in the distance, warning of heavier rainfall soon.

Dove stands from the bed, immediately dizzy the moment her feet hit the ground. But she soon recovers and shuffles slowly to the window, pulling a blanket off her bed. It trails behind her like an elegant ballgown's train. She wraps it around her shoulders and pulls it tight.

She loses herself watching the raindrops as they roll down the windows. Two, six, fifteen, and then she loses count as they merge and fall and disappear. Two raindrops race down the glass, collecting other drops as they go. She stares at the right-hand droplet, keeping track of its progress versus the left-hand drop. Dove doesn't know what the winning conditions are, but she still smiles softly when her drop reaches the end of the window first.

As she stares, other students walk across the wet cobblestones in the courtyard. They have umbrellas in their house colors, or slickers with the hoods pulled over their faces. One student is running, a book on top of their head. As if that would protect them from the rain.

She watches them, thinking about the enormity of the differences between them and her. How she used to be just like them, and how one moment changed everything for her. How easy it was, she realized, to become "other." It could happen to anyone, at any moment. It happened to her so quickly.

It makes her jaw ache. She's not bitter that it happened, but that others don't understand the swiftness of change. That the same thing could happen to them. Maybe not in the same way, but it didn't matter.

Her hands ball into fists on the windows as she watches the bustle below her. She doesn't want to be angry that her life has turned out this way. But the universe, and maybe the Goddess, seem to do everything in their power to make her that way.

The door opens and she jumps. She hasn't been watching the time—how long has she been standing at the window, lost in her own thoughts?

Rory has returned with a bag of something that smells heavenly. Dove's stomach grumbles in anticipation as Rory shakes out her umbrella in the hallway.

"It's raining so hard out there," she says by way of greeting. "I hope the food is still warm."

"It smells amazing," Dove says, sniffing the air. She takes the bag from Rory, who is trying to shake off her coat as well.

They sit on the floor together, stuffing their faces with a spread that could feed at least five of them, but Dove is content. She watches Rory, happily chewing away at a sweet roll and licking her fingers between each bite.

"Thank you," Dove says softly. "I'm—" She stops, unsure how to say what she's feeling. A thank you simply doesn't feel like enough. Maybe for the food, but not for everything else Rory has done for her.

Rory regards her with soft eyes, her head tilted slightly to the side. She sets the sweet roll down, licking the last of the frosting from her fingers and wiping them on a napkin before planting her hands on the floor between them.

"It's hard to break like that. I did when Mom…" She swallows, gaze drifting to the floor. "It never gets easier, Dove. You only learn to live with it. You learn to adapt to your new normal. But it doesn't mean you don't deserve help while you're figuring it out."

"But why are you doing it for me?" Dove asks, unable to stop herself.

Rory's smile is as beautiful as always, but it doesn't reach her eyes. "Because no one did it for me. I can't stand that for someone else."

Dove's heart squeezes painfully. If she thought Roan had been excellent at hiding his pain, he was nothing compared to Rory. She'd taken that pain and turned it into kindness—it took a very special sort of person to do such a thing. And here she was, fetching her sweet rolls in the rain, sitting on the floor with her, and stroking her hair to get her to sleep.

Dove knows she is staring, openmouthed. She forces her mouth closed and picks up a flaky pastry with raspberries, breaking off a corner and stuffing it into her mouth. She doesn't know what else to say.

Thank you isn't enough.

Rory doesn't seem to mind as she picks her sweet roll back up and digs back in. "By the way," she says through a mouthful, "one of the chancellor's staff stopped by this morning right before you woke up. The chancellor would like to see you. Whenever you're ready to go."

Dove stops with a piece of pastry halfway to her mouth. Was it about the incident in the dining hall yesterday? Did the chancellor really think it had something to do with Dove? Was she in trouble?

The logical part of her told her that no, she wasn't. If she was going to get in trouble for it, they wouldn't have given her a loose timeframe. They would have demanded her out of bed and to the chancellor's office immediately. But they'd given her time, allowed her the chance to eat breakfast with Rory and contemplate her existence at the window. She didn't think that was necessarily the motivation behind the request, but it didn't matter.

"Thank you." She's said those words so many times in the last few minutes that they feel unreal, like she's made up words to substitute for the real ones, whatever they might be.

She watches Rory, her heart full of something effervescent. The sensation is a tickle in her ribcage, a falling cerise bloom inside her chest that is as welcome as a light breeze in summer. She wishes she could capture it in a bottle and revisit it when she needed a reminder that good things still existed. And this was because of Rory, because of her kindness, because of her presence. Dove wouldn't let her go easily.

"Would you maybe want to come with me?" Dove asks, the words spilling from her lips. Her face heats. "Just to walk me to the office! You don't have to come in or anything, I don't even know if the chancellor would let you in. But I just think I'd feel more comfortable if you were there and I know you probably have other things to do but—"

Rory laughs, holding up a hand to stop Dove's rambling. "Sure, I'll walk you there." Her smile is huge, crooked, and perfect.

7

———

AEGIS

*D*ove's stockings are soaked by the time they reach the chancellor's office. Although she has her umbrella, the rain is falling sideways.

When they arrive, Rory takes Dove's umbrella with a gentle hand, throwing her a crooked smile. "You'll be fine. Nothing to worry about. I'll be here when you're done."

Dove releases a long breath, exhaling her anxieties as best she can before turning to push open the huge wooden door.

The chancellor looks up from her desk and waves her in. Her yellow hair is still curled softly, but it seems flatter, frizzier, as if the chancellor didn't have time to fix it before arriving at her office that morning. Dove takes in the slight bruise-colored shadows beneath her eyes her glasses cannot hide. This definitely *isn't* a good sign.

"Please, have a seat." Chancellor Brigaine gestures to the leather armchairs Dove is too familiar with at this point. "Would you like some tea?"

Dove thinks if she tries to drink anything now, she may throw up. Or possibly faint. Her stomach is churning like a boat on a very tumultuous ocean, and she can't fathom the thought of adding more to it when it's already this turbulent. She shakes her head.

The chancellor looks at her over her glasses, her eyebrows raised. And although she seems calm, Dove senses a tension in the air that wasn't present before, even after her Revelation Ceremony.

A door opens somewhere behind her. Dove glances around and a woman whose sea storm hair she would recognize anywhere appears.

Hyacinth.

If she's here, Dove is definitely in trouble. They will no doubt blame her for the incident in the dining hall last night. Her heart races in her throat while she imagines her life in the island's secluded prison. She'll be forced to spend her days bored, being educated on the ways her wrongdoings have impacted their society, how she should be grateful for the chance to have lived here. She won't see the sun except through a tiny barred window at the top of her cell. She will always be cold, shivering under threadbare blankets.

Dove knows nothing of the actual conditions of the prison. A tiny voice in the back of her head scolds her for dramatizing, but the images persist, nonetheless.

Hyacinth simply gives her a soft smile and sits beside her in the opposite armchair. Her navy coat drapes elegantly over her knees, her boots shined to a polish so high, Dove swears she can see Hyacinth's reflection in them.

"Miss Cita, please, relax. You aren't in trouble."

Dove jumps at her voice and looks down at her hands. She is gripping the chair arms so tightly her nails leave half-moons in the soft leather. She breathes in, then releases them slowly on the exhale.

She turns her gaze to Hyacinth. "What do you need

me for?"

Hyacinth tents her fingers on her knee. "I'm glad you asked. There is something we need to ask you about."

The chancellor adjusts her spectacles. "I want to stress that you are not in trouble, although your involvement with the matter has brought some"—she frowns, pursing her lips—"complexity to the issue."

Dove's heart does not calm at the words. Her insides are still a mess of nerves, roiling and rocking back and forth inside of her. She can't control them. Her hands tremble, even as she clenches them together in her lap. She hopes Hyacinth doesn't see them.

Hyacinth nods. "The issue, Dove, is that there has been a case of the Drain here on campus."

"The Drain? Isn't that..." Dove trails off. There hasn't been a documented case of the Drain for hundreds of years—she thinks. There has never been a case on the islands during her lifetime, of that she knows for sure.

"A disease we thought exterminated long ago," Chancellor Brigaine says, shaking her head. "But there is no other explanation for what happened to this student."

The memory shivers through her. The way his hair had been streaked with grey. He'd looked pale. Had that really been the Drain? Were they all in danger? She didn't even know how the disease spread or how they could protect themselves from it. She didn't know if there was a cure, either. They'd wiped the disease out, sure, but she didn't know how they'd done so.

"You had an altercation with Lapis," Hyacinth continues. "His friends insist you had something to do with his affliction."

"I would never!" Dove cries, holding her hands in surrender before her. "I could never do such a horrible thing to someone, no matter what they'd done to me!"

72

Chancellor Brigaine sighs, her expression softening. "Circumstances are never as straightforward as they may seem, Miss Cita. But we believe you did not knowingly cause his affliction."

Dove's mind snags on one word—*knowingly*. She wants to ask, wants to understand what the chancellor meant by that. She hadn't fought with Lapis, at least not physically. All she'd done was run away.

"Did you see him again after your argument yesterday?" Hyacinth interrupts her catastrophizing, taking notes in a small pocket handbook, her pen scraping on the page.

"No, ma'am. I didn't see him again until he collapsed in the dining hall."

She listens to the pen scratch on the paper and watches Hyacinth's neat handwriting. The patter of rain on the window of the office rattles melodiously, an uncoordinated beat to the steady rhythm of Hyacinth's pen. Each scratch rattles in her chest, every stroke a tally carved into her skin, announcing that she is wrong, wrong, *wrong*.

Small bracelets on her wrist rattle as she shivers. She's not cold.

"May I ask," Dove says, breaking the silence, "why my encounter with Lapis complicates this matter?"

Hyacinth's pen stops scratching. The chancellor shifts uncomfortably in her seat. Dove looks from the chancellor, to Hyacinth, and back again. Her heartbeat travels to her throat once more, unbidden.

Hyacinth twists her pen closed, tucking it into her breast pocket and closing the miniature notebook. "Before we had the research capabilities we do now..." She trails off, eyes flicking over the stacks of books as if she is searching for something. "Many believed the colorless to be a portent, of sorts."

Dove recoils. "A portent of what?"

"Many things," the chancellor says. "And none of them verified, Dove. But we have noticed a…pattern, so to speak. With the appearance of the colorless, the Drain reemerges too."

Hyacinth cuts in. "The Aegis Order takes precautions, of course, but without solid evidence of correlation, we can't cause widespread panic with unverified claims."

Dove can't breathe. Her chest is tight, weighed down with breaths she cannot take but so desperately needs to. "You're afraid I might Drain a mate," Dove realizes, breathlessly. "That's why it's forbidden."

Hyacinth's lips are tight, a thin, white line across her sharp features. She says nothing, but she doesn't have to. Dove can read the silence between the two women before her.

"There's a possibility I may have Drained Lapis unknowingly." The realization strikes Dove like a blow to her gut. Horror creeps through her veins—she doesn't know how the Drain spreads, or how she might have had a hand in Lapis' affliction.

Hyacinth looks at the chancellor. Their expressions mirror one another, and Dove can't interpret them. Her eyes are burning. Dove squeezes them shut, a vain attempt to keep the tears from escaping. The rustle of cloth announces someone's approach.

"Dove." Hyacinth's voice is gentler than Dove would expect. "The hospital is taking care of Lapis. The Aegis Order is investigating. We know you wouldn't do this on purpose."

But Dove opens her eyes and sees the way Hyacinth won't touch her. That nagging voice in the back of her mind reminds her that Hyacinth is just being cautious— but her heart screams for comfort. Comfort she will never be allowed, not anymore.

She doesn't know what comes next. She doesn't even know what the next few minutes will hold. But Hyacinth looks at her gently, her face serious and kind all at once. She gives Dove a small smile, then taps the chair arm twice.

"Your studies should remain your number one priority, Miss Cita," the chancellor says.

Dove bites her lip. That's all she's truly ever wanted from Prism Academy, anyway. To understand the history of the island. To learn things about her world she wouldn't know otherwise. Her studies were always her priority. But it is still a comfort to hear the words from the chancellor. She bobs her chin, unable to speak but grateful all the same.

Hyacinth sighs. "We would caution you not to share this information with others. It would be unwise to spread false information when we do not know all the facts. For now, keep your distance as best as you can from other students."

That was already the plan forming in Dove's mind. She needed to be vigilant, even more than she ever had been before. It was only when she'd let her guard down that she'd run into Lapis.

She nods again, eyes on the floor. She won't make the same mistake twice.

When she leaves five minutes later, a grim twinge of determination has settled in her bones. She must prove herself, her innocence, her purpose in the world. If her soul color will not grant her that, then she must build a life despite her lack.

She runs bodily into Rory, nearly knocking her over and crashing their heads together. Rory curses softly and Dove stumbles, grabbing onto the wall for balance.

"I'm sorry," Dove pants as she grips the wall.

Rory shakes out her head, then rubs her forehead where Dove can see a small red mark forming. "Where are you off to in such a rush? How did it go in there? Is everything okay?"

Dove doesn't know how to explain what is happening in her mind. The fear that she is most likely the cause of the Drain, the way Hyacinth wouldn't touch her...

Touch. Hyacinth wouldn't touch her.

And she'd just run into Rory. *Touched* Rory. She let her guard down again, immediately after swearing she wouldn't. She doesn't know how the Drain spreads, what causes it, and if she might be at risk. She doesn't understand what sort of threat it poses. But she has already broken the promise that she made to herself, to Hyacinth, not to touch another student.

Rory watches her with an odd expression—one eyebrow lifted and a slight downturn to her lips. "Dove?"

She knows she must look harried in Rory's eyes. But she doesn't know how to set any of this to rights. Rory can't know about what she talked about with Hyacinth and the chancellor, after all. The only thing Dove can tell her is to keep her distance; an odd request even with context.

"I need to finish some assignments. Let's go to the library." Dove turns and doesn't wait to see if Rory follows.

Footsteps follow behind her. "Dove, wait! You didn't answer—"

Rory's hand stops on her shoulder, and Dove ducks away almost instinctively from it. Her heart is beating faster than she thought possible, painfully thrashing against her ribs.

She takes a few more steps, then turns to Rory. She can't meet the other girl's eyes, and instead keeps her gaze on the flagstones beneath their feet. "I can't tell you."

"You could have said that instead of running away, you know." Her words are a gentle scold, but her tone is soft. Like she can sense that whatever happened in the chancellor's office was too much for Dove.

Dove sighs. "I really do need to go to the library." She finally lifts her gaze to Rory, whose eyes are softer than Dove has ever seen them. "You coming?"

Rory's lopsided smile spreads. "Of course."

She beckons Rory to follow, retrieving her umbrella from Rory's grasp as they head out of the administrative building. She follows Dove without a word, opening her umbrella when they step out into the rain and carefully avoiding puddles.

The library is, by far, the most beautiful building on the Prism campus. Three stories of floor-to-ceiling bookshelves and elegantly carved railings frame tall, peaked windows where the rain streams down in rivulets. The marble floor is a combination of white and grey marble, shot through with the occasional vein of gold.

The first floor is home to a series of beautiful woven rugs playing host to wooden tables for students to use as workspace. The second and third floors are entirely dedicated to stacks and stacks of books. A massive marble staircase zigzags up to the third floor, and each bookshelf is home to many wooden ladders on wheels and rails. A desk stands in the corner by the entryway with an older man sitting behind it, hunched over a book. Behind him, a card catalog cabinet stands imposingly tall. A woven rattan cabinet stands beside it, a golden lock glittering in the diffused light.

The librarian's hair is ash blonde, streaked with gray, and a pair of spectacles sit low on his nose. As Dove approaches, he looks up, his violet eyes meeting hers with a dreamy look, as if he hasn't quite come back from wherever he was while reading.

"I need everything you've got on the Drain," Dove says as soon as she reaches the desk. She grabs the wood with both hands, nearly throwing herself over the surface as she stops her momentum so suddenly.

His eyebrows rise, and he looks at her with a touch of disbelief. "The disease?"

She nods, vigorously. He frowns, but shuffles to the collection of cards in the small drawers, pulling on several of them in succession. She shifts on her feet. Rory is beside her, and Dove can feel her stare.

He muses for a few seconds, tapping his chin and humming, until he finds what he is looking for and pulls open a drawer about halfway down. Inside, Dove can see a series of small paper cards, each with a tab at the top. From here she can't read what they say, but she assumes it has something to do with her query.

Rory is quiet while they wait, but Dove thinks she must want to ask. But Dove can't explain now, not while there are too many unknowns. Her heart weighs heavily in her chest and she glances sidelong at Rory. Her expression seems neutral, but there is a miniscule pinch between her eyebrows.

The librarian scratches several titles on a sheet of paper. Dove is practically vibrating, anxious energy building to a pitch inside her as she waits.

"Start with these," the librarian says, and slides the

paper across the desk toward her. He raises a single, bushy eyebrow. "And please walk while you're in the library."

She finally meets the librarian's gaze and exhales an embarrassed laugh. "It's that obvious, huh?"

He chuckles. "Very much so. Best of luck."

She thanks him profusely as she takes the paper, forcing herself to walk slowly through the marble archway into the first floor of the library. She finds an empty table and sets her damp bag down on the floor.

Rory follows her to the table but doesn't move to sit or set her bag down. Instead, she stares at Dove, following her almost manic movements with slightly narrowed eyes.

"Dove," she says, softly. "Wait. Before you go on this library craze. What happened with the chancellor? What are you trying to find?"

Dove meets her gaze, Rory's wide blue eyes settling the agitation in her chest to a gentle rumble. She sighs, then pulls a chair out to sit. There's no explanation that could cover everything inside of her right now, but Rory deserves something more than blind faith.

She clenches her hands on her lap. "Remember that boy we saw yesterday? Something has apparently infected him with the Drain."

Rory recoils, her mouth dropping open. "The Drain? But wasn't that eradicated?"

"Apparently it's back, or so the chancellor says."

"But what does it have to do with you?" Rory shakes her head, sitting across from Dove. "They can't think you gave it to him, do they?"

Dove shrugs. "They don't know. But I want to find out, if I can."

Rory frowns, the expression as lopsided as her smile, but infinitely less charming. Dove doesn't know why the look bothers her. The urge to say something, anything, to get Rory to stop frowning builds inside her throat, like a bit of fruit stuck in her windpipe. It's almost painful. But she swallows it down and sets the paper from the librarian between them.

She describes as much as she can to Rory—how she isn't sure of the way the Drain spreads, or how little she knows of the colorless. How all she wants is to prove that, beyond a doubt, she had nothing to do with Lapis' infection. Dove knows she's breaking the promise she made to Hyacinth, but it's impossible to keep anything from Rory.

Especially not when her frown has finally turned into something better. Rory rolls her lip between her teeth as she stares at the list. She points to a few of the titles with a pen and tears off the lower part of the paper to write them there.

"I'll get these." She waves the ripped scrap in front of Dove. "You get the rest. Yeah?"

Dove nods, then Rory spins away, her curls fanning out behind her.

Dove meanders through the stacks, fingers brushing over the worn leather spines. She loves the smell of the library—old leather, dust, warmth. It's hard to describe accurately, hard to pinpoint exactly why it makes her feel like she's wrapped in a warm blanket.

It's also home to thousands of books, containing millions of different pieces of information. She thinks the sheer amount of knowledge contained here is overwhelming. But it's a beautiful thing to have it at her hands like this.

Especially, she thinks as she pulls the first title down from a high shelf, if it helps her prove she isn't a walking plague.

She spends another half an hour searching until she

can barely hold her stack of books. She totters down the stairs, having ventured up to the second floor for a few of the tomes. The stack is tall enough that she can't see around it, so when she reaches the stairs, she feels tentatively before her for the next stair.

Her foot slips—she gasps as she falls, gripping the books even tighter. She braces for impact, but it never comes. Instead, a strong arm grasps her around the waist.

"Your research must be fascinating to carry this many books at once." The voice is unfamiliar.

A blond boy is smiling down at her, one large hand on the top of her books. His eyes are like a pure chunk of citrine, golden and molten and huge.

"Uh, thank you," she stammers, regaining her footing as best she can while trying to calm her embarrassed blush.

He keeps a hand on her back until she's steady again, then takes some books from her stack. "I'll carry these down, so you don't slip again."

She has no time to protest before he's gone, heading down the stairs at a clip. She takes off after him, tucking the remaining books underneath her arm. He doesn't slow for her, but he stays in her vision, steering toward an empty table on the first floor.

He sets her books down, then turns toward her with a wide smile. "There. Safe and sound, no injuries."

She thunks the rest of the books on the same table and turns to him, mouth tight. "Thank you for your help, but…"

He holds out a hand to her. "Jasper. Yellow house." His house was obvious enough from his brilliant yellow checkered pants.

She doesn't take his hand, but smiles. "Dove. Green house."

He takes her hand anyway, shaking it vigorously. "Nice to meet you, Dove." He pauses, still holding her hand. "I've heard about you."

She freezes, nerves roiling in her gut. Was he going to harass her now that he knew who she was? Was she in danger? Her insides are hot, overriding the logical part of her brain telling her she was fine here, there were lots of witnesses, the librarian surely wouldn't let someone hurt her here. She yanks her hand away like his skin burns.

"You're the colorless girl, aren't you?" He says, but his tone isn't like that of the boys that harassed her. It's curiosity, not hostility, that colors his voice.

Dove still doesn't respond, biting her tongue as she gauges the best way to handle the situation. She doesn't know what to do—does she acknowledge it and possibly invite trouble? Does she lie and deny it?

"I—" she begins.

"Dove?" Rory's voice is smooth, soft.

Dove's entire being is forced back, like a moon pulled into orbit. This is new—the sensation of her body, her *soul*, being pulled toward Rory.

Jasper's open expression doesn't change. He shifts his gaze to Rory and nods. "She nearly fell down the stairs earlier."

Rory's beside her now, a smile tugging at the corners of her lips. "Yeah? I was just wondering where you'd gotten off to. You've been gone a while."

Her cheeks flush, but she holds her head up. "I might have overestimated how many books I could carry."

"She definitely overestimated," Jasper says.

Rory laughs, then takes the books beneath Dove's arm. She nods to Jasper, then points at the rest of the books on the table. "Grab those, Dove. Thanks for helping her, Jasper."

Jasper bows his head. "Happy to. Be careful, you two."

Dove mumbles a thank you and an apology all at once, so the words come out as a jumble, but Jasper seems to understand. He waves as she leaves, his smile as warm and sunny as his uniform.

Rory grips Dove's free hand, pulling her back toward their table. Dove allows this with no protestations, anticipation building in the space between their palms. All she can hope is that the books provide them with some answers to her questions.

8

——————

FAMILY

*D*ove's first week at Prism Academy is less exciting than her first day had been, much to her relief. It puts her at ease that most of the students at Prism seem inclined to stare and gossip rather than take action. She can handle a few odd looks and the occasional whisper. But violence…violence is something she cannot take.

Roan also appears more during her day than she expected. He's there when she leaves class in the literature and humanities buildings; their breaks seem to coincide often; and once, when she stopped by the library to grab a book for her ancient literature course, he was there, hunched over a textbook larger than her torso at a table with a comically small lamp.

Rory is still asleep when Dove wakes on their first day off school. She pads around the room softly, slipping out of her night clothes and into a blue sundress with flounce sleeves. It is one of her favorites, one her mother had helped her pick out.

Her mother, who is coming to visit today. Both of her parents, actually. And they'd have to talk about her soul color.

She is dreading the conversation, and not because of the reaction she thinks her parents will have. She is ashamed of her failure, and facing her beloved family when she has no color is a shame she cannot bear quietly.

Rory doesn't stir as Dove sits at her desk, shuffling a half-finished paper and a book—its place marked with a ribbon—aside and pulling her small mirror toward herself. She applies dried cerise blooms to her lips and cheeks and brushes a small bit of shimmer powder on her eyelids.

After she finishes, Dove stares at herself in the mirror. What is she hoping for—a sign the mirror was wrong? Maybe a miracle that her desk mirror somehow has gained the same powers as the Aura Mirror?

The impossibility of it leaves a sour taste on her tongue. She pushes the mirror back into place and shakes her head.

Rory stirs a few minutes later, groaning. When she sits up, her curls are frizzy and unruly, and she blinks blearily in Dove's direction. The morning sun has only just hit her bed; it shines on her curls and gilds the side of her face.

"Good morning." Dove smiles. Rory will either ignore her completely, or, if she's feeling kind, will grunt in her general direction.

It seems this morning that Rory is outgoing, as she grunts once before laying back down and yanking the covers back over her head. If Dove lets Rory sleep any longer though, she may miss her family.

Dove's face falls as she thinks about Rory's family— her mother, gone from a mysterious illness. Her father, left in mourning for his soulmate. What will family day look like for Rory? For Roan? Will they spend the day watching the other families as they parade around campus, laughing? How will Rory see Dove and her family together? Will she be sad? Jealous? Dove wouldn't blame her if she was. But she still can't let Rory miss family day, regardless of what it may or may not look like.

Dove stands and heads to Rory's bed, pulling the covers down enough so that Rory's face is drenched in sunlight. Several sleep-mussed curls have fallen across her face, and a few more stick to her forehead. Dove gently brushes them away.

"Rory," she whispers as she tucks another stray curl behind her ear, "come on, it's time to wake up."

Rory mumbles something resembling words. Dove thinks it may have been *leave me alone*.

She gently takes one of Rory's shoulders and shakes it. Not hard, but enough to jostle the girl's head on her pillow.

Rory groans again, swatting pitifully at Dove and missing completely. Dove smiles, unrelenting in her gentle attempts to wake up her sleeping roommate. Rory eventually cedes, opening one eye just a crack to give Dove the meanest glare she's ever seen.

"Whaddya want?"

"It's family day. You wanted time to get ready."

Rory groans for a third time, but this time she opens both eyes and sits up. The covers slide down, and her hair is a mess, but she's awake. Dove smiles at her again and stands, gesturing for Rory to get up.

"I'm going, I'm going," she whines, but there's a hint of a smile in her voice.

Their morning bustle is a routine Dove finds much comfort in. Moving around each other with a grace already learned in a week of sharing a small, confined space. Knowing where the other left an item they can't find on their own. Understanding what different sounds of frustration mean. She may have grown up an only child, but Dove thinks this must be what it's like to have a sibling.

When Rory is finally ready, they give each other an appraising once-over, checking for smudged lipstick, a stray lock of hair, or a misaligned sleeve. They nod to one another and head for the door.

Families of the newest class of Prism students will meet them in the science hall, the largest lecture building on campus. Dove catches a glance at a clock as they head down the stairs. Many of the families would already be there; midmorning had already come and gone.

Dove hooks her arm around Rory's and pulls, urging her to move faster.

Rory laughs, letting herself be dragged along. "Dove, stop, we aren't late."

The lecture hall is a cacophony of noise—the squeals of young children seeing their beloved older sibling; the sounds of parents greeting their students with loving words; the din of hundreds of different conversations that are all somehow eerily similar.

Dove does not see her parents immediately upon entering. Rory, however, finds Roan almost instantly, standing next to a tall man with grey curly hair, piercing ocean blue eyes, and a crooked grin just like his children.

Rory squeals, then folds herself into her father's arms. She melts into him like she is made of ice in a heatwave. He returns the enthusiasm, kissing her head and squeezing her tightly.

Roan catches Dove's eye and smiles. She doesn't want to interrupt, and she has her own parents to find. She gives Roan a small wave. He returns it, then shoos her away. *Go,* he mouths.

She obeys.

It only takes another few minutes to find her own parents, and when she does, she finds herself unable to hold back her tears upon seeing them.

Her mother stands beneath an archway in the back of the room, her arms crossed over her chest, flame-red hair tied in a plait that rests on the side of her neck. Her father stands beside her, leaning against the column and looking as if he just got done reading an interesting newspaper article. His glasses are halfway down his nose, but he pushes them back up when he spots Dove.

"Lovey!" her mother practically screams as she rushes to her daughter and clings to her, shushing Dove's cries as she buries her face in her mother's chest. "Oh, little bird, it's alright."

Dove grips her mother with every ounce of strength she has in her, knotting her hands in her mother's blouse, not caring if she wrinkles the fabric. Her mother pets her hair softly, running one hand from the crown of her head down to her mid back. She's wrapped the other around Dove in a grip that would squash her in any other circumstance.

But right now, Dove needs that grip, that crushing love that only her mother can give her.

"Dovey love, do you want to go somewhere more private?" her father whispers, his face near her ear.

Dove's mother releases her enough to look up, but not completely. She keeps a hand on Dove's hair, cradling the back of her head. Dove nods to her father, the action rubbing her hair against her mother's smooth, delicate hand.

"Why don't you show us your dorm," Dove's mother suggests. "We can talk privately there."

Dove nods again, and her mother lets her go, but grabs her hand before Dove can move away. Dove squeezes—

her mother squeezes back.

Their trek across campus is silent. Dove only watches the cobbles as she walks, their patterns etched into her consciousness from too many days spent staring at the ground. Her parents follow closely behind. They know the campus, though things may have changed since they attended when they were her age. But it doesn't matter—they aren't here for a tour.

When they arrive at the Green dorm, Dove hardly looks behind as she ascends the stairs and unlocks the room. The sunlight streams through the gap left in the curtains pulled over the tall windows, a golden halo in which motes of dust float lazily. It mocks her—it looks just like her soul did in the mirror.

She sits unceremoniously on her bed as her parents file in behind her. Her father shuts the door quietly while her mother takes a seat on the bed next to her. Dove's tears have stopped, for now. But they prickle at the corners of her eyes and she knows the moment any of them speak, she won't be able to stop them.

Her mother rubs her back with a gentle hand, smooth circles over and over. It's her father who speaks first.

"Dove, we heard about your color from the Order," he says. His tone is soft, kind, almost apologetic. "And about your being unable to take a mate."

She predicted it right—the tears roll down her cheeks. Her mother reaches up to swipe some tears away with her cool fingers. "Oh, my love," she coos. "I can't imagine what you must be feeling right now."

Dove gasps, the tears hot on her face. "I've let you down."

"Oh, little bird, no. You haven't. We could never think that."

Her father strides across the room and crouches

before Dove, enveloping her hands with his own. They are big and warm and remind her of all the good things about her life before she found out she was colorless. All the love and joy she had before everything was taken from her.

Her mother's hand hasn't left her back, but the other is now resting atop her father's hands, the joining of all their hands in her lap creates a knot of love that Dove focuses all her energy on.

"You are still our daughter, Dove, no matter what your soul color is," her father says. "You are brilliant and bright and beautiful. We love you more than anything in this world."

"And we couldn't be more proud of you," her mother adds. "You've handled this with grace and strength. Your spirit is like iron."

Dove lifts her eyes to her father's face. Their eyes meet—his are deep, nearly black, with a touch of gold near the center. But the look in his eyes says all she needs to know. They aren't lying to her when they say they are proud, when they say they love her.

"I was—" she hiccups. She breathes a few times and regains her composure. "I was so afraid you would be ashamed of me."

Her father squeezes her hands again. "There are very few things you could do that would make us ashamed of you. Something out of your control is certainly not one of them." He releases one of her hands, then touches his fingertip to her nose, something he used to do often when she was very little. "Now, mooning people at the beach, on the other hand…"

She laughs wetly. When she was three, she hated most clothes and would often strip them off in rebellion. On a family beach trip, she chose an inopportune time to rebel in such a way. It was a memory her father would occasionally tease her about when he wanted her to laugh. Now the memory rests warm and soft in her belly, like the first hot sip of tea that heats your body from within. They aren't ashamed of her. They don't see her as a failure.

The thought is as gentle as the grip her father still has on her hands. His fingers are not delicate but worn and calloused from years of weaving and working with thick fabrics. She has always known her father's hands this way. To Dove, they are home.

"Lovey," her mother says, stroking her hair again, "there are so many things in this world that people will try to tell you will determine your worth. For as much importance as we place upon soul color, it doesn't determine who you are. It doesn't determine who you want to be." She smiles, then gently takes Dove's chin in her fingers. "Only you, my sweet girl, get to choose that. Who you are, who you will become, is entirely up to you."

The tears are hot on her face again, but these aren't tears of shame like earlier. Dove doesn't know how she got so lucky to have parents like hers. It was almost as if the Goddess was apologizing for giving her a colorless soul. As penance, she made sure Dove was raised in a household that would give her nothing but love, regardless of her hue.

It was a lesson, she supposed, from the Goddess. A lesson that no matter what color her beautiful mirror would show, all people she created were worthy of being loved. Even those with no color.

She folds into her mother, nuzzling into her neck and letting the cerise blossom scent of her sink deep into her memory. "Thank you," she whispers. Her mother simply holds her.

That evening, she glances frequently at the door, waiting for Rory to return. Her parents left nearly an hour before. She's been alone with her thoughts since.

They spent nearly all of family day in her dorm room, consoling Dove's fate and discussing the implications of her not being allowed a mate. In the end, her parents could do nothing—it was a directive from the Aegis Order. She couldn't fight it, no matter how much she wanted to.

She'd been comforted when they commiserated in the surface-level unfairness of it all. But deep down, she understood the missive. After all, why would they want there to be more colorless souls like her? There were no guarantees about the color of her children's souls.

Dove is on her bed; her lilac frilled lounge pants bunch around her knees as she tries her best to read a book for class. Although she's read the same sentence at least seven times now, she can't accept defeat and put the book aside. If she does, she will be alone with her thoughts.

The lock turns and Dove jerks upright. Rory is back, much to her relief.

Her head enters first, through the crack between the door and the frame. Her curls fall to the side, a dark waterfall against the light wood, and when her eyes meet Dove's, she smiles.

"Oh good, you're still awake." She opens the door the rest of the way and sidles into the room, a canvas bag slung over her shoulder that Dove doesn't recognize. She follows Dove's gaze and grins. "Dad brought some clementines." She shrugs the bag off her shoulder. "Want one?"

Dove nods. Rory tosses her one, and Dove nearly drops it, fumbling it into the front of her shirt. Her bungling of the fruit prompts a laugh from Rory, and it's such a bright sound in Dove's ears.

She digs her fingernail into the rind and peels it back, relishing the fresh citrusy smell that immediately wafts up to her nose. It is lusciously sweet, and Dove imagines the way the fruit will burst against her tongue with the first bite.

The bed shifts, and Rory plops down next to her. "I thought you might need some cheering up." She gestures to the rest of the clementines still in the bag on her lap. "Have as many as you like."

Dove pops a piece of clementine in her mouth, the sweet juice coating her tongue. If Rory's goal was to cheer her up, this had certainly been a good way to do it.

She hums in contentment before swallowing to reply. "Thank you, really. These are my favorite."

Rory beams, then grabs a fruit from her lap for herself. "My dad said the Order gave you some…bad news, huh?"

Dove pauses in the middle of peeling off another slice. She doesn't know what Rory's father does for work, but he must know people within the Order if he's heard about her being denied a mate.

Rory must take her pause as embarrassment or fear; she hurries to speak before Dove can form the words to explain. "I—I just mean that he heard from one of his seniors about it and he asked me because he knew I was your roommate and—"

Dove cuts off her babbling. "Rory, does your dad work for the Aegis Order?"

Rory nods. "I didn't tell you that already?"

"No, but it's okay. What did he hear?" she asks, but

she already knows what the news must be.

She watches Rory busy herself peeling her clementine slowly; the skin comes off in perfect ribbons. Her fingers are slow and meticulous; her eyes never leave her hands as she works.

"That you—" she clenches her jaw and peels a bit more of the fruit. "You can't take a mate. I mean, that can't be true. They couldn't do something so cruel to you!"

Dove says nothing. She watches Rory finish peeling her clementine, then shred the perfect peel into tiny bits. The citrus scent is thick in the air. Dove doesn't want the smell associated in her memories with something so painful. But something in it brings calm.

Dove bites her lip. "It's true. But I understand. They can't guarantee I won't pass my colorless traits onto my children. It's easier to stop it all together."

"But they won't even let you love someone? You don't have to make"—she flushes—"*babies*, you know. You can just agree not to reproduce!"

"They can't risk it. There are too many unknowns."

Rory huffs, tossing her perfectly peeled clementine onto the bed between them and then throwing her hands in the air. "That makes no sense! It's just cruel to determine someone's life like that over something they can't even control!"

It was sweet for Rory to get so angry on Dove's behalf. She isn't used to someone doing this for her—but no matter how furious Rory gets, it won't change anything. The Aegis Order's word is law. Just like her parents can't change her fate, neither can Rory.

"You're really kind, you know. No one would think to get angry for me."

"Why wouldn't I get angry?" Rory lists her head to the side, drawing her brows together. "It's unfair—anyone would be in my place."

Dove smiles and shakes her head. "No, they wouldn't. You're…something else."

Rory picks her discarded fruit off the bed and grabs a slice. She pops it in her mouth, lips puckering at the sweetness. Dove watches her with a mix of gratitude and admiration. Their meeting may have seemed like chance, but she is convinced it was the Goddess guiding them together.

They finish their fruits on Dove's bed, giggling and trading slices and eating more when the first run out. Dove thinks that even if she can't find a mate, that having someone to be there for her like Rory has just might be enough.

9

———

RESEARCH

*D*ove has a new idea—after her frantic search through the library last week, she found very little about the Drain in any of the books the librarian had recommended. Everything in them she already knew.

But, according to the chancellor and to Hyacinth, the colorless had something to do with the spread of the Drain. Maybe the answers she seeks will lie in history books. If the Drain exists, that must imply the existence of colorless souls in the past. If she can find more information about her condition, maybe it will lead her to more information about the Drain.

Her existence hadn't surprised the chancellor and Hyacinth; although she'd never learned about the colorless in school, their lack of shock over her condition implied knowledge of it, even if it wasn't widespread.

Dove hefts her bag over her shoulder and steps into the library. The midmorning sun shines on the marble floor and illuminates the endless stacks of books. The scene invites her in, as if the sun itself is encouraging her to find what she isn't even sure is here.

She approaches the librarian behind his desk once

more and smiles at him. He's not paying attention to her, not right away. He concentrates on the large tome before him, a finger gliding over the page as he reads.

"Excuse me," Dove says, quietly.

His finger pauses, and he glances up, his glasses sliding down his nose as he does. "Welcome back. What can I help you with?"

"I'm looking for some history books—ones about soul colors, please."

He smiles. "Certainly. Any specific color you want to focus on?"

"The…" She trails off, looking down at her hands on the desk. She imagines her hands leeching the color from the wood, leaving it as blanched as the rotting pieces of driftwood on the beach. "The colorless, if possible."

The librarian doesn't reply, only nods his head incrementally. He stands, leaving the book open on his desk, and shuffles to the card catalog. Just like the last time, he scratches several titles on a sheet of paper for her and lists their location in the stacks. When he hands her the paper, his eyes are crinkled slits, like she has stumbled into a joke only he understands.

"Start here," he says. "I've listed a few titles here that should be a good place to begin, but there are many others that may prove useful. If these titles don't help, please do come back and see me again. I have many other suggestions I can give you."

Dove bows her head again in gratitude and begins her search for the first book on his list. It's titled *Irisium Historel*, and is apparently on the first floor. Just her luck.

She wanders through the stacks, eyes trained high on the very top of the shelves. The sun hits them just right, their golden rays dripping down the mahogany wood like honey on a biscuit.

Dove finds the stack the librarian wrote on the list and turns down the space between the shelves. Her book is located halfway down the stacks, tucked between other historical texts with fading silver and gold titles on their spines. She spots several copies and pulls the oldest one from the shelf.

If she's going to find something helpful, she will need to go as far back into history as she can. After all, the lack of knowledge about the colorless must mean it hasn't happened for a very long time.

She's lost in thought, breathing in deeply as she flips the book open right there in the middle of the stacks.

"Dove?" A quiet calling of her name. She nearly drops her book in surprise.

When she turns, Roan is there, leaning against a shelf, arms crossed over his chest. She snaps the book shut, harder than she meant to, and tucks it under her arm. "Roan!"

He smiles at her, blue eyes twinkling, then tips his chin at the book. "Research?"

"Something like that."

He pushes off the stack, his smile deepening. "I've got a table. Care to join me?"

Dove adjusts the book as she nods. He turns, taking a few steps away before looking at her over his shoulder. Roan cocks a finger at her, beckoning her to follow. She complies.

Roan's table is in the furthest corner of the grid of tables in the library's foyer. Materials are spread across half of its width, open books and loose sheets of paper scattered in a storm of frantic academia. He pushes some of it over into a smaller pile and gestures for her to sit in the newly cleared space. Dove sets the book down and drops her bag to the floor.

She opens the book to the back and searches the glossary with one finger running over the rough pages. Colorless, Solum Iris, anything that might help her. She can't focus though; Roan is staring at her, laser-focused.

She whips her head up to meet his gaze. "You're staring."

Roan blinks, surprise washing over his features. "I... am?" He shakes his head, rubbing his hands over his eyes. "I'm sorry, Dove, I didn't mean to. I'm exhausted. I must have zoned out."

Dove softens. "It's okay. I'm just having a hard time focusing." She throws him a soft smile.

He huffs a laugh, dipping his head toward his chest. "Maybe I should get going then, so you can focus on your research." He tilts his head to gaze at the title she retrieved. "History?"

She nods and meets his eyes. "Take a nap, maybe?" Roan's hands are splayed on the table in front of her. Before she can consider it further, she reaches a hand out to pat his.

He stares at her hand on top of his for some time, watching it like a cat might consider a bird. But the moment is gone as quickly as it comes, and soon he is withdrawing his hands to push back from the table.

"You're right," he concedes, standing. "Will you be alright?"

"I'll be fine. Go. Get some sleep."

He sighs, dropping his shoulders. He bows to her with a hand over his heart and sets to gathering the scattered papers and books. She catches glimpses of the titles and frowns. Several are familiar; in fact, they are the same ones the librarian listed on the paper for her research into the colorless.

Roan focus is history, this much she knows. But for

him to be studying the colorless as well...is he doing it for her?

"Roan...what were you researching?"

He shrugs, nonchalant. "Early island civilization. Soul color origins."

She wants to ask why, but the words get caught in her throat. Roan shoves the rest of the papers in his bag and stacks the books. When he reaches to scoop them into his arms, she puts a hand on top of the books.

"You can leave them." It saves her a trip, at least.

He cocks an eyebrow at her but doesn't protest. He just takes his hands away from the books and shoots her a wink before retreating.

She watches him go, hand still resting on his stack of books and the question melting on her tongue. Why was he researching the same thing as her? Was it a simple coincidence, or had he heard about Lapis?

Paranoia has her glancing around at the other students scattered throughout the library tables. None pay her any mind; no one glances her way or whispers behind their hands. Either they are very good at hiding their curiosity, or they truly don't know.

Then how did Roan? If he *did* know, which wasn't guaranteed.

Dove shakes her head and pulls the stack of books toward her before reopening her first book to the glossary once more. She has work to do; she can't worry about Roan and what he does or doesn't know.

Dove spends the next three hours researching the history

of the magic of soul colors. What she finds is nothing new.

The Goddess, thousands of years ago, plucked a red, a yellow, and a blue feather from her tail and used them to create the very first people. She then created the Azura Isles for her children to live upon. She gave them the ocean, the air, and the soil to live upon, and told them the colors given to them were a gift of her love. That they should do all they can to protect those colors.

From those original three, six more were created. One Red child, one Yellow child, and one Blue child. But also, one Green, one Orange, and one Violet child.

Soon, the Azura Isles were filled with people with a rainbow of soul colors. As a gift to her people, the Goddess blessed the Yellow's mirror with her magic, allowing her creations to see their soul colors without her help.

And then, the Goddess disappeared.

But the people of the Azura Isles never forgot the gift their Goddess had given them—their souls. They protected these colorful pieces of themselves and created a society meant to protect their integrity and brilliance.

But not a single book, not a single passage, mentions the existence of color variances. None mention the anomaly that is her colorless soul.

She slams the last book shut with a groan. These books aren't helping. The information she finds is stories she already knows, things she was taught when she was young. There is nothing new.

But there are other books on her list, and the librarian said if she didn't find what she needed, she could always come back to him. This was only the beginning of her research. If she gave up now, she would be pathetic, a quitter.

She returns her book and the ones Roan left to the cart by the librarian's desk, keeping only one that she hasn't had the chance to read yet. It probably will contain even more of the same stories that Dove already knows and information that won't help. But she won't rest until she's exhausted all her resources.

The kind librarian watches her return the stack of books, a bushy eyebrow cocked. "How did those titles work out for you?"

She meets his gaze, then drops it back to the books she is arranging on the cart. "I didn't quite find what I was looking for, unfortunately. But your recommendations were helpful."

The librarian nods, then hands her another sheet of paper. More titles and locations in the library are written on the paper, and he nods again when he slides it across the desk to her. "Here. I've put together some more recommendations. It'll take you a while to get through this list, but they are here when you are ready."

She takes the list, scanning down the list of twenty-some titles and her chest tightens. Such kindness from him. His charity is exceptional, and she doesn't know if she is special or if this is simply how he is.

Dove bows her head to him. "Thank you. This will be very useful in my research."

He flaps a hand at her. "Just doing my job, child."

"Still, thank you." She tucks the paper into her bag, folding it with the first sheet he gave her. She's already checked off the books she read today, but it never hurts to reference them again in case she missed something.

She turns to leave, still carrying the final book from her morning haul. First lunch, then a return to the library for even more research.

"Dove," a voice cuts through her planning. When she glances up, she's met with a pair of golden eyes she's seen before. The boy who'd saved her from slipping is back, and smiling widely at her. "Your stack is reasonable today," he continues, gesturing at the book in her hands.

She doesn't know how to respond, so she just laughs awkwardly. What was his name again? Jade? Beryl?

"Jasper," he says, his smile no less brilliant than it had been moments before. "I figured maybe you forgot, with all that happened."

A blush rises to her cheeks, her embarrassment hard to hide. "I'm so sorry Jasper. It's been..." She trails off, unsure how to describe what she's experienced over the last few days.

He shrugs good naturedly and sets back off toward the stairs, gesturing for her to follow. "I don't mind, really." He looks at the book in her hands and cocks an eyebrow. "Medicine before, now history? Trying to decide on a focus?"

Dove shakes her head. "I'm studying history, but you know how research can be." She watches Jasper from the corner of her eye, weighing how her attempt at nonchalance lands with the boy.

He doesn't seem to notice, continuing with fervor. "I'm in history, myself. Always found the history of soul colors and the disappearance of the Goddess to be interesting."

Dove frowns. Maybe he could be of use? If he's spent some time researching the exact thing she needs help with, it couldn't hurt to ask. "I was just researching a similar topic. Any tidbits or myths you'd be willing to share?"

Jasper laughs. "All of it is speculation, if you really want to know. Most texts regarding the Goddess are, anyway. It's been over a thousand years since she disappeared—anything from that time has long turned to dust. We have no reliable sources of information beyond speculation and a few pieces of really nice pottery."

Dove's frown deepens. Just when she thought she'd

had something...

"But I did read something interesting about the colorless. That's why I asked about you so bluntly last time." He gives her a small bow. "I'm sorry about that, by the way. That was rude of me."

"No!" She protests, desperate to keep them on the subject. "It didn't bother me, really. If you don't mind, can you tell me about what you read?"

Jasper winks. "I'll do you one better—I'll give you the book the passage was in. How's that?"

"That would be excellent. Thank you, Jasper."

He stops and stares for a moment, listing his head to the side. She doesn't know what he's staring at, but the heat rises to her cheeks again. With no way to stop it, she turns her head away.

"I thought so," he says finally, chuckling. "You're the prettiest when you're smiling."

Somewhere in the back of Dove's mind, she knows he's flirting with her. But how does one respond to such advances? She has no experience in this. Breath is stuck in her chest, expanding beneath her ribcage, unstopping.

Jasper turns from the grand doors of the library, from Dove, and walks away. Dove doesn't follow, doing her best to release the pent-up air stuck in her lungs. If a simple compliment has her completely immobilized, maybe it is for the best that she is forbidden from finding a partner. Or maybe, she muses wryly, it is *because* it's prohibited that she is reacting this way.

She lifts her gaze to the arched ceiling, silently begging the Goddess to give her strength. The gentle creak of the library doors echoes beneath the quiet buzzing of students, and a glimpse of red hair catches her attention. It's Roan, returned from his nap and looking less vacant than before. He flashes her a smile but does not stop.

Dove squeezes her eyes shut so hard she sees stars.

Only when she hears footsteps does she reopen her eyes. Jasper is back, holding a book in his hands with a curling, gold-leaf script on the front. His smile is gone, replaced with a wide-eyed expression that Dove can only interpret as worry.

"Are you alright?" he asks, holding the book to his chest.

She must be terrible at hiding her expressions if Jasper is reacting to her like this. He must sense something is up without her needing to say a word. She couldn't tell him it was because of him, that would be ridiculous. But how could Dove explain what was happening inside her head without explaining all that had transpired before this?

She settles on avoidance, instead. "I'm hungry, is all." She points to the book. "Is this the one?"

He nods and hands it to her. "Please, read it for yourself. And let me know if you have questions, okay?"

Dove takes the book from him, staring down at the cover titled *Color Theory*. She runs a gentle hand over the title, tracing its elegant script absently. "Thank you, Jasper. You're a wonderful help."

"Don't mention it."

She can't peel her eyes away to look at him—whether it's fascination or embarrassment she doesn't know. Unbidden, Rory's face appears in her mind's eye. What would she make of the situation, of Jasper's flirtations? Would she flit Dove away, like she did in the dining hall? Or would she encourage Dove to explore, even if it was forbidden?

She doesn't notice when Jasper leaves, only that she is alone when she finally looks up.

10

———

WARMTH

Dove spends the next two weeks holed up in the library with every free moment she has. Rory sometimes joins, but never stays as late into the evenings. Dove pretends not to notice the lingering stares when Rory leaves, but it's harder than she expects to ignore.

Dove finds information about the Drain that scares her—it is indeed a formidable disease, claiming its victims not in death, but in spirit. A victim loses all their color, eventually draining their soul to its dregs, leaving nothing behind but a shell of the person they once were. Victims end up dying from related complications: starvation, dehydration, and other avoidable causes. Modern science has all but eradicated the disease, supposedly.

But what Dove can't figure out is why it's back or what is causing it.

It is a sunny afternoon when Rory finally breaks their studious silence. She slams her book shut, rattling the table. "I'm hungry."

Dove doesn't lift her head. "You don't have to stay."

"Come with me." A huffing breath, and a chair scraping across the floor. "The books will be here when we get back, Dove."

Dove shakes her head. "I'm fine."

Rory goes quiet as Dove returns to her reading. Footsteps sound against the marble flooring, but fade into obscurity as she continues scanning down the page.

The Drain has always been associated with the colorless—this much she already knows. But why do the colorless happen? Why does the Drain appear when a colorless soul appears? The books do not answer her questions, only give her more of the same about the Goddess' colorful gifts and her disappearance.

When a hand touches her shoulder, Dove nearly jumps out of her skin.

Rory's stare is harsh, at first. Her eyebrows crinkle in a way that sends Dove's heart fluttering. But then she softens, her hard edges turning hazy in the golden lamplight of the library. Her hand turns delicate and travels to grip Dove under her chin.

"Take a break. Please."

It's the first time Dove has heard her ask so courteously. She has always known Rory as the biggest energy in the room; this change of character is abrupt and startling. Enough so that Dove finally shuts the book before her with a soft *thunk*.

She nods, and Rory's soft fingers fall away from her chin. In the absence of their warmth, her skin prickles.

They don't head to the dining hall. Instead, Rory drags her to a small coffee cart that sits at the edge of the lake by the weeping willow. She points to one of the wooden benches beneath its tresses. Dove waits and watches, breathing slowly to calm her nerves and take in the willow's beauty and the lake's gentle waters.

The sunlight moves on the water like fireflies in a

dance; she's entranced by it, following the ripples as a soft breeze ruffles the water and sends the light scattering across its surface. It's like watching the women who dance in prayer for the Goddess every week, movements fluid and light, airy and mesmerizing.

She's read so much about the Goddess in her research, but she still doesn't understand. Although the Goddess seems connected in every way to every piece of the island, Dove cannot accept how she, in her colorlessness, exists. Why did the Goddess not bless her with the same gifts she gave all the others? Was Dove somehow a disappointment? Had she done something to not be worthy of the Goddess' gift?

Dove shakes her head. It is a pointless endeavor to worry about the Goddess now, so long after she disappeared. Whatever caused Dove's condition, it was determined long before she existed.

Rory places a steaming cup into her hand, wrapping Dove's fingers around it and smiling. Dove meets Rory's eyes and still doesn't feel like she has returned to herself. Rory's eyes sparkle in the afternoon light, the same way the light dances on the lake.

"Strawberry latte," Rory says, glancing at the cup in Dove's hands. "I figured something sweet might help."

Dove looks at the cup. A small pink heart floats on top of the sweet cream, and she can't stop the smile that tugs at her lips. "Thank you, Rory."

Rory snorts. "I'm just glad you're out of the library." Her expression turns serious, then. "You were scaring me."

Dove takes a sip of her drink and bows her head to Rory. "I didn't mean to—"

"Dove!" a voice calls from across the courtyard.

She turns from Rory to find the source of the sound. A student in red pants is jogging toward them, waving his hand frantically in the air. It's Roan, looking windblown. He skids to a stop before them and collapses over his knees, bracing himself as he pants heavily from exertion.

Rory rolls her eyes good-naturedly. "Winded from a light jog?"

Roan waves a hand at her but can't muster the strength to speak just yet. Rory nudges him with the toe of her Mary Janes. He smiles wryly at her, lopsided as it rises and falls with his breaths.

"Sorry," he finally manages between breaths. "I was running laps—I haven't been able to check on you, Dove, since the library."

She grips the cup tightly, staring down into the pink foam heart. "I'm fine, Roan. Thank you."

"And am I a rotting fish carcass?" Rory protests, stabbing her finger into Roan's ribs. "You haven't checked up on *me*."

Roan rolls his eyes, smile never fading. "You don't need me to check on you."

"And Dove does?"

Dove sips her drink, leaning back on the bench and watching the siblings quietly. She can't stop the curve of her lips as they squabble, their expressions mirrors of each other. They look so alike, from the arch of their brows to the way they stand. Dove suspects if she points these similarities out to them, they would protest.

Rory clears her throat loudly, then reaches toward Dove. "We were actually just taking a break, but we should probably get back to what we were doing," she says, glaring at Roan as if to say, *don't follow us.*

Dove obliges and stands, but she glances back at Roan as they walk away. He watches her, and when he catches her looking at him, he winks.

They don't return to the library like Dove thought—Rory takes her around campus instead. They weave their way through the main campus buildings and Dove tries to focus on something other than the research waiting for her at the library.

Rory glances over her shoulder as they round a corner by the greenhouse. "We can go back after this. I just wanted to show you one more thing."

Dove nods, and Rory gestures toward the greenhouse door. Dove has no classes in the building and nothing nearby, so she's never been over here. The greenhouse is beautiful, made of fluted glass and metal, its roof also see-through. A sign hangs on the front door, depicting a hand-painted flower vase that says, "Open."

Rory tugs her inside, and Dove can't hold back a gasp.

Inside, the greenhouse explodes with color. Flowers of every shade battle for her attention, woven between thick strands of ivy and brilliant leaves of the purest green. More ivy ropes its way around the ceiling, too, and airy bits of moss hang dramatically, like a curtain.

Rory breathes in deeply, closing her eyes and tilting her head up. Dove watches her. The way her throat curves elegantly, outlined by the filtered sunlight. The way a stray curl stays tucked into her shirt collar. She hasn't considered it enough, but Rory is incredibly beautiful.

The sunlight here is soft, filtered through the moss and vines on the ceiling and gives the greenhouse a dream-like quality. It's as if Dove is seeing the life before her through clouded lenses.

Rory's eyes meet Dove's. She doesn't know if she

should turn away, but the burning on her cheeks is strange.

"Beautiful," Rory says, then looks around. "This is my favorite place on campus. I sometimes come here between classes."

Dove's hands are cold on her burning cheeks. "It's peaceful, like a dream."

"I think so too."

They stay there for what Dove swears is hours, weaving their way through the tight walkways between benches. Plants spill into the aisles, densely enough that when Dove passes by, leafy tendrils brush over her arms.

She doesn't even know where to look. Her head swivels as they weave; she spots a brilliant orange flower with black stripes, then her gaze jumps to a pink and white plant with holes in its leaves. There is simply too much to see, too much to take in. But it isn't overwhelming—it's an adventure. The longer they spend, the more she relaxes.

A bush of blue petaled flowers explodes with rich hues, and Dove stares, entranced. Did the Goddess make everything in their world as colorful as she made her people? Is this cacophony of color and loveliness by design? If not created by the hand of the Goddess, then nature must have seen the elegance of the Goddess herself and sought to mimic it.

A flower catches her eye on the bush—it is devoid of color, the blue that touches the rest of the flowers nowhere to be seen on its delicate petals. But it isn't ugly by any means. It has flowered just the same as the rest of the bush, its petals soft and pointed at the tips.

It has not suffered for its differences. If anything, Dove notes, it has flourished. She softens. She reaches out to stroke the petals, gentle yet tentative.

Rory pulls up to another door, turning back to meet Dove's wonderment. "Ready?"

The trance is broken. She pulls her hand away from the white flower and nods to Rory, letting her lead Dove from the greenhouse and back across campus.

When they return to the library, their things are behind the librarian's desk. Other students have taken over their table; in fact, all the tables in the library are occupied now.

The librarian hands their things over with a knowing smile. "I've noted you'll be borrowing these," he says, sliding the books across the desk. "Best of luck."

"I know you'll just say it's your job but thank you anyway."

The librarian smiles, cheeks rosy. He doesn't respond, but Dove suspects he's holding back his usual retort.

They make their way back across campus, light waning as they reach the Green dorm. Rory holds the door open for Dove, and they ascend the stairs to their room together. The books are weighty in Dove's arms, not because they are thick, but because she feels their importance like many stones. The knowledge contained within them is a tidal wave that she is sure will change the course of her life, just as much as the revelation ceremony changed it first.

Maybe she is putting too much hope in simple text; maybe there is less within than she believes. But if she doesn't hold on to the hope that she will find the key to her colorlessness, what is the point of trying?

Rory is there, unlocking their door with the key attached to her necklace. Rory, the blockade against the rush of change, her defender against the storm. Dove watches her wrist as she turns the key. It is delicate, beautiful, and smooth. The Goddess must have known what was in store for her; in response, she sent Rory.

A Goddess-send. That is what Rory is for Dove. A

light in the darkness, a warm embrace when she is too weary to continue. Because she has Rory, Dove will be fine. She'll make it through to whatever is next. No matter her soul color, Rory is there for her.

The thought fills her with warmth.

11

BEACH

The trip to the greenhouse reinvigorated Dove. But the need for information nags at her. It eats away at her compulsively, ebbing at the back of her mind like the persistent ocean tides.

She dreams of soul colors. Of the mirror, of Rory, of Roan, and of the massive doors to the chancellor's office. There is the kind librarian's smile, her own reflection in the high shine of Hyacinth's boots.

And every single time, when she wakes from her dreams, she cannot fall back asleep.

In her classes, she takes notes. Scribbles the snatches of phrases she can comprehend. But when she returns to them later, she cannot decipher what she has recorded. It's as if the need has taken over her and made her into a monster she doesn't remember.

So, when she finally has a break, she gathers the books loaned from the library and settles in for a long day of research. After all, if her dreams returned, she wouldn't get much sleep. She might as well use her time properly.

Dove settles at her desk, pushing aside crumpled papers, fountain pens, and dried inkwells. Her hand hits something hard.

She lifts the papers and stacks them beneath the book she has uncovered—*Color Theory*. The book Jasper gave her. The one that, until right now, she'd forgotten about in the frenzy of her research. She slides a hand over the cover, tracing the gold-leaf letters absently.

"Let's go out," Rory declares suddenly, bashing through their door with great force.

Dove nearly falls from her chair. "Bleeding colors, Rory!"

Rory sweeps across the room, her entire body radiating determination and confidence. She holds her chin high as her curls bounce with each step she takes. When she reaches Dove, she leans forward over Dove's shoulder.

"You deserve a break." Rory taps Dove's chair, hair brushing against the side of Dove's neck. "And I won't take no for an answer."

Azura guide her. She knows Rory means well, but a break will only put her further behind in her research. And she can't afford distractions, not when so much is at stake.

Dove shakes her head and returns to *Color Theory*, pulling the book toward her without a word.

Rory stands, flinging herself backward onto Dove's lavender bedspread and sighing. "Please? It'll be fun." Her eyes are wide, child-like as she pleads with Dove. The blue is brighter than ever, as if her very soul is begging for Dove to come along.

She is very hard to resist.

Dove sighs. "Alright, fine. But I get to say when we come home, okay?"

Rory brightens, her spine straightening. She nods vigorously and stands from the bed, hurrying to her closet.

She packs an oversized woven bag with the essentials, gesturing for Dove to do the same.

They pass the same campus sights she's grown to love—the willow tree with its maudlin branches sweeping gracefully across the grass; the coffee cart that Rory dragged her to earlier that week; the alleyways between buildings shrouded in shadow but never ominous.

Even if Dove's place in society is a question, she belongs here, at Prism. Even though she is colorless, even though her soul is like glass, Prism fills her with light.

Dove hasn't been to the beach since that first day at Prism—the day she learned of what happened to Rory and Roan's mother. How she'd faded like a ghost, drained of all color...

They round the last corner to the beach as realization takes Dove by surprise. She gasps, stopping in her tracks. Rory returns her vocalization with a quizzical look, a dark eyebrow raised beneath her curly bangs.

"Dove?" is all Rory says, frowning.

Dove shakes her head, her floppy hat bouncing. Her mind is frantic, like leaves on an autumn wind. They pass too quickly to grasp and the full picture scatters, inconclusive as to its shape.

The theory that tickles the edges of her mind is dark— that the Valerus siblings lost their mother to the Drain.

If she is right, then it means that the boy who assaulted her wasn't the first case. That there may be more people affected by this disease right now. That the Drain isn't just contained to one person, to her. And she has absolutely no idea how it spreads.

Dove knows that this isn't her responsibility; the Aegis Order exists for reasons like this. If the Drain is indeed spreading, they already know. They must.

And there's no way she can propose her half-baked

theory to Rory. It would only reopen old wounds, ones that she'd obviously worked for years to nurture and heal. Dove couldn't live with herself if she were to open them again.

Rory stares, concern and confusion seemingly waging a war with her eyebrows. The wrinkle between is deep, a crease that Dove knows has been worn away at over time.

"Are you okay? Should we go back?" Rory says quietly. "Did you hurt yourself?"

Dove shakes her head, the bow on her hat swaying. "I'm fine." She shoulders her bag with determination. "Let's go enjoy the beach."

Rory nods, but as they walk toward the sandy shore, Dove knows Rory's gaze is fixed on her.

Rory spreads a blue and white checkered blanket on the sand and tugs at the corners. It's far from the water and beneath a tree, partially shaded by large leaves. She plops onto the blanket with little ceremony, pulling her bag open and taking a pair of sunshades out.

Dove joins her, tucking her knees underneath her as her skirts flow out. *Color Theory* is still tucked away in her bag. Dove resists the urge to grab for it right away—Rory is still staring at her. Like she knows there's something Dove isn't telling her.

But Rory doesn't ask. She rolls up the legs of her pants and runs across the sand; the sun glistens in her hair like a thousand golden beads cling to each strand. Dove watches the way her stride kicks up sand like tiny explosions, how the water flows around her ankles when she splashes into it. Something about Rory's carefree nature strikes a chord in Dove.

She knows some of what Rory has been through, but what Dove doesn't understand is how she can be so untroubled. Or appear to be.

Rory spins to face Dove, the rolled hems on her pants wet from the ocean. "It's the perfect temperature, Dove!"

Dove smiles. She can't help it. It parts her lips without her bidding it to do so, splits her open and unfurls everything she's keeping inside. Like Rory is the sun, and she is a flower desperate for every drop of light she can get.

She abandons her book, joining Rory in the ocean's spray.

They play like Dove has not played in years; Rory kicks water at her legs, soaking Dove's skirts and giggling wildly. Dove finds a sea star and gestures frantically for Rory to come see. Schools of tiny silver fish weave around their legs when they stand still, racing away in a metallic wave when Rory wiggles her toes.

And when Dove has exhausted herself completely and flops back on the towel, the sun dries the salty water on her legs. It evaporates and leaves a flaky second skin that itches.

Rory collapses beside her, the particles of sun weaving through her curly hair and reflecting off leftover droplets of water. Rory *shines,* and something flutters up in Dove's throat, a need to touch her, a need to weave her fingers in between the light, to wrap Rory's light with her own. It's like Rory was built to shine in all of Dove's empty corners, the ones with no light at all.

"Dove?" Rory says, breaking her focus. "You alright?"

She is anything but. She doesn't know what this urge is, this starved desire that sits in her chest and screams at her to lean in. But she tamps down on it and stifles it. This is not the time.

She nods to Rory instead, crossing her arms behind her head and laying back. Rory says nothing more. Dove is hyper-aware of Rory's body next to hers, but she says still.

They lay in the shade for some time, of which Dove quickly loses track. Before long, Rory announces she is going to collect shells, and Dove doesn't follow. *Color Theory* is calling her name. She's played enough—it's time.

She opens it to the first chapter, titled "The Goddess," and begins to read.

Nothing is new here—it's the same information she's learned over her many years of education. The Goddess and her gift, then her sudden disappearance.

The subsequent chapters describe soul color theory itself. How each soul color appears in people of certain personalities. Red is the color of leaders and revolutionaries, people with big dreams and the fortitude to back them up. Blue is the color of the peacekeepers, the dreamers, and the teachers. And yellow, the last primary, is the color of the ambitious and kind, the ones who want to make the world a better place.

Secondary colors present themselves in people with mixes of these traits. People aren't only their colors, of course, but something can be said for a shift once people discover their colors.

Does discovering someone's soul color make a person more likely to fall into the traits their color represents? If that's true, what will happen to her? If her soul is nothing, what kind of person will she be?

She shakes her head, pulling her attention from her thoughts. Jasper said there was something in here about the colorless—she should focus on that, shouldn't she?

She flips to the table of contents, skimming it for what she needs. There is a chapter titled, "Solum Iris." She remembers what Chancellor Brigaine said the day of the Revelation Ceremony. She doesn't know what it means.

Dove thumbs through the pages and finds the chapter. As she reads, something inside her flutters. She expects whatever lies in these pages to change her life significantly. Or maybe that's too much pressure to put on a single chapter of a single book. Maybe she's hoping for too much.

Her eyes snag on the definition she's been looking for. *Solum Iris—the lonely rainbow.* Apparently, colorless are named as such because of light color theory. While not the same as soul color theory, old color scientists believed that light color theory influenced soul color theory. Although more studies have shown color theory to work differently for souls, the name stayed.

Because in light, all colors create white.

Dove pauses, her finger marking her spot on the page. In light, all colors make white? She's hollowed by this, her insides vanishing into a void of disbelief. If only that were true. If only she were just like Rory, with all the colors inside of her.

But she's not. Soul color theory is different—the book says so, her teachers say so, every class she's ever taken about science and art have said so. The colors the Goddess gave her children don't work the same as the colors of the world. Otherwise, by now, everyone would have black souls.

"Find anything?" Rory says.

Dove jumps, surprised from her intense focus by Rory returning, hands full of white and brown shells. She looks up, head spinning. Rory smiles down at her with that lopsided grin Dove loves so much. She tries to react, to give Rory something in return.

Rory doesn't press—instead, she crouches down in front of Dove and gestures for her to hold out her hands. Dove obeys. Rory lays a single shell, swirling and white, streaked with veins of purplish brown in her palm.

"It's an amethyst snail shell. They're hard to find intact like that."

Dove looks closer at the shell. It's beautiful indeed, no bigger than her thumbnail and pointed at the top. The grooves are deep and twisted, creating a swirling, bumpy pattern up the top of the shell.

Rory gestures again with a finger. "Look inside."

Dove turns the tiny shell over and looks inside. It is empty—but the color left behind is nothing short of stunning. It sparkles in the sunlight, pristine and deep purple as the stone from which the animal takes its name.

Dove turns it over again, looking at the charming little shell from all angles. It's lighter than a feather, so small Dove is afraid if she breathes too hard, it may fly out of her hand and back into the ocean.

Rory busies herself by putting the rest of the shells on the towel to air dry. There are so many, but none like the amethyst snail shell she gave Dove. Rory smiles down at her collection on the towel.

"Keep that," Rory says, gesturing her chin at the tiny shell.

Dove stares at the shell, then meets Rory's gaze. "I couldn't—"

Rory stops her with a raised hand, shaking her head. "It's a gift. You can't give it back, that would be rude."

Dove wants to laugh and cry all at once. Rory collapses back, and Dove returns her gaze to the shell. There is so much *more* Dove needs to do—research to conduct, theories to prove, and a soul to color. The ever-increasing list of tasks is daunting.

But she can't deny this crash against her chest. The feeling that this shell means more than she knows, than Rory knows. That there's something more here, and that Dove has no interest in stopping whatever it is.

12

VITREOUS

*D*ove knows she doesn't *have* to do this. But the what ifs would eat at her for the rest of her life if she didn't. And when she asked Roan to accompany her to visit Lapis in the hospital, he readily agreed.

Having Roan will make it easier. She has to know. She needs to confirm if her theory is correct. Because if Roan and Rory's mom really passed from the Drain...

Well, Dove wasn't sure *what* she would do.

He's waiting for her when she emerges from the Green dorm, leaning against the brick wall and watching the sky. Roan smiles broadly when he spots her, kicking off the wall to meet her. Dove returns the expression.

Roan slings an arm around her shoulders, "How are you feeling today?" His tone is light, but there's an undercurrent of something there. Worry, maybe?

"I'm fine," she replies, gently ducking away from his arm. She wants to say more, to assuage whatever fear he's feeling. She isn't doing this because she wants to apologize to Lapis—or at least not entirely. Even though he was cruel to her, she never wished for this kind of harm to come to him.

His arm drops. He says nothing, and Dove offers no more. If he really is going to take issue with this trip, he can say something on his own.

They leave the Prism campus, crossing over the bridge to downtown. Streetcars huff by as Dove sidesteps pedestrians and Roan follows behind. She senses that same nervous energy from him, radiating and pulsating as he trails her between the crowds. But he says nothing. Maybe she's overthinking it.

The hospital is a conglomeration of several square brick buildings smashed together. It gives Dove the impression of a haphazard, frantic construction done quickly out of necessity. She's never been here before, but she knows of it, as it is the only hospital on the four Azura islands.

Roan urges her toward the massive stone staircase and steps up, turning back to offer Dove a hand. She hesitates. Roan waits patiently, his expression soft and unreadable.

"It's a long walk up," he says gently, and extends his hand a little further toward Dove. "Nothing inappropriate, I promise."

She has enough to worry about today. A helping hand should not be one of those things, but it must be. She shakes her head, and Roan drops his hand slowly.

They ascend the stairs and tiny stones crunch beneath Dove's loafers. She has to watch her feet, careful not to step wrong and bring Roan crashing down with her. The walk is indeed not a short one, but by the time they reach the top she is confronted once more by the reality of why she is here.

A boy is *dying* from the Drain, and she needs to know if it's her fault.

The hospital is quiet when they enter. A solemn sort of air folds around Dove and presses down. Her feet are heavy, too heavy to lift, too heavy to even wiggle her toes. She is rooted to the spot at the entrance.

Despite her earlier protests, Roan takes her hand anyway. "Dove," he says, voice impossibly gentle. "We can leave if this is too much. I wouldn't blame you."

She *has* to go. She can't stop now. Rory would have understood, but Roan... Roan wasn't there when the boy collapsed. Roan only saw him at his worst. He didn't see the way the life faded from his eyes, how his hair turned grey.

Dove shakes her head and takes a steadying breath. "No, Roan." She exhales, the puncture of her breath through the air sharp. "I have to do this. I must."

Roan lets her hand go. He says nothing more, but Dove senses his tension. Worry for her, no doubt.

The nurse behind a reception desk has been watching their exchange. When Dove steps up to the desk, she smiles gently at Dove.

"How can I help you, dear?" she asks. Her voice is warm, soothing, like lemon tea with a bit of honey.

Roan explains, and the nurse nods. She leads them down the hallway and up a flight of stone stairs. The hospital is bright, Dove notices when she finally allows herself to look somewhere other than her own feet. Large windows flank their ascent and the bright sunlight floods through and illuminates the stone in brilliant patches of butter yellow.

Lapis' room is on the second floor. The door has a small window, cut just large enough to see if someone waits behind. The nurse opens it gently and calls out to the boy laying in the bed, still as death.

"Mister Nero? You have visitors," the nurse says in her soft voice.

The boy does not stir.

The nurse turns to Roan and Dove, nodding her head. "I'll leave you two here, then." She gestures at a small bell by the door. "Ring this if you need a nurse."

Roan bows his head. "Thank you."

Dove can't muster up the words. They're stuck in her throat, lodged deep in her windpipe. She tries, but chokes on air. Roan simply places a hand on the small of her back as the nurse leaves the room and closes the door with a click.

She's afraid to turn back to the bed. Afraid to see what waits for her there.

Roan steps away, letting his hand fall away. She's left with a cold spot instead, one that spreads up her entire back and prickles the hair on her neck. It's a sensation she'd do anything to avoid again.

She forces herself to turn. She has to do this—she owes it to herself, to the school, to Rory and Roan and everyone else who might yet believe in her. She needs to understand more. And to do that, she has to face this.

Dove's teeth hurt. She's grinding them, hard, as she steps up to the bed. Lapis lays, still as death, beneath the sheets. His once deerskin colored hair is now white, blanched like the sands of the Azura beaches. She can see his eyes move erratically beneath the thin skin of his eyelids. He's dreaming—but with their violent dance, Dove isn't so sure he's not having a nightmare instead.

Hovering at his bedside, she breathes. In and out, slowly, so slowly. She doesn't want to wake him, and for what she needs, she doesn't have to. Roan stands by the door, unwilling to interrupt or come any closer.

The boy's hands are by his sides, clenched into fists and gripping the sheets ferociously. A sheen of sweat glistens on his forehead. Guilt churns in her stomach but for what she doesn't know. She didn't do this to him—the

Drain did.

Dove turns to Roan and gestures for him to come closer with a gentle crook of her fingers. He hesitates, brow furrowed in indecision. But after a moment of still deliberation he steps closer. Joining Dove by the boy's bedside, the crease between his eyebrows only grows deeper.

She isn't sure how to broach the subject with Roan. *Does he look like your dying mother did? Are these symptoms you recognize?* She realizes, too late, that this might be a traumatic experience for Roan. She's so *stupid*, she thinks, for dragging him into this. He agreed to accompany her, sure, but she didn't warn him what she wanted him here for. He must have assumed he was here for moral support. Instead, she has dragged him along to reopen old wounds.

Didn't she avoid asking Rory this very same question to preserve her heart? Why is she doing the same thing to Roan?

What an awful person she is.

But Roan stays, steadfast, at her side, gazing down at the pale boy in the bed with a look she can't begin to name. Her heart stutters.

"Roan," she whispers, knowing what she's about to say is too little too late. "I'm sorry if this brings up memories…"

He squeezes his eyes shut at her words. Silence settles between them, heavier than a stone. It sinks into Dove's stomach. She's never seen Roan make an expression like this. And it's all *her* fault.

Roan shakes his head. "I'm fine, Dove."

"I'm sorry," she says again.

He frowns deeper. "You did nothing wrong. I volunteered to come with you."

"But you look so stressed—"

A groan from the bed cuts the rest of her sentence short.

Dove's heart stutters into her throat, choking off her words and sending her scuttling back from the bed to the bell by the door. She doesn't even know if a nurse is necessary, but she doesn't want to be alone in the room when he finishes waking up.

A nurse appears just as the boy's eyes flutter open. They take in Roan first, then slide to Dove. When they find her, Dove can't help but gasp softly.

They are entirely white, save for the dark, mottled gray of his pupils. It is unnerving to see them, like a ghost has sucked all the boy's color dry. There is a faint ring of blue, as if the last traces of his color are clinging to life.

A nurse brushes past Dove with a murmured apology and comes to stand at the boy's bedside. She busies herself around the bed, adjusting dials and checking the needles in his arms. Dove watches with wide eyes, fearful she has done something wrong.

Roan moves out of the nurse's way to come by Dove. He places a hand on her shoulder, squeezing gently when she tenses at his touch. He's being comforting, she knows, but her gut will not stop squirming. She knows this isn't her fault, but her heart refuses to listen to logic.

The boy's gaze moves to Roan, even as the nurse bustles around him. She adjusts the drip and Dove watches as the boy's eyelids grow heavy once more. It takes several minutes of awkward silence for him to fall asleep, eyes never leaving Roan.

When he finally slips back into sleep, the nurse sighs and turns to Roan and Dove. "I'm afraid he won't be awake for your visit," she says, shrugging. "The disease saps most of his strength—we find it's best to keep him asleep more often than not."

She moves to leave, but Dove stops her. "Wait!"

The nurse stops, her lips pinched and brows drawn. She says nothing, only waits for Dove to continue.

Dove remembers all she learned from the chancellor, from the library and her research. She can't leave without confirming the details—the spread of the Drain and its supposed cure. Can the boy be healed? Does her colorless soul really have something to do with his fate?

"If you don't mind," Dove breathes, trying to speak slowly over her pounding blood. "May I ask a few questions about the Drain?"

The nurse softens. "Of course. Let's speak in the hallway so we don't disturb him."

Dove and Roan follow the nurse from Lapis' room. The door closes with a definitive *click* behind them, and something in Dove releases. A tension she didn't realize she was carrying, like a weight she was holding finally released. The tension in her stomach, the roiling nerves of guilt and apprehension though, they do not fade even as she leaves the room behind.

The nurse gestures to chairs along the wall opposite the door, upholstered in a thick brown woven fabric. Roan waits for Dove to sit before doing the same. The nurse turns her gaze to Dove, her deep burgundy eyes alert and waiting.

"What would you like to know, dear?" she asks.

Dove breathes deeply, the scent of the hospital— antiseptic and vinegar—fills her nose. "I know there hasn't been a case in a long time, but...how does the Drain spread? Is it contagious?"

The nurse shakes her head. "Thankfully, the Drain has not been observed as an airborne contagion, at least not from the records we have from the last outbreak.

This is the first confirmed case we've seen in more than a century. Contracting the disease comes from—" She clears her throat, looking purposefully at Dove. "Well, we suspect it comes from prolonged or purposeful contact with the colorless."

The shudder travels up her spine. She's lost for words by the statement, though. The colorless really *do* cause the Drain. Then it *was* her fault—after all, there are no other colorless in the Azura Isles other than her, as far as anyone knows. It must have been during the fight. The boy somehow contracted it from her then.

"What does that mean," Dove begins, "prolonged or purposeful?"

The nurse gives her a knowing smile. "Well, often activities such as hugging, kissing, and holding hands are considered prolonged or purposeful. It was hypothesized that repeated contact, even if brief, could produce similar infection results. So even if it were several kisses over a few weeks, it would have the same effect."

Her theorizing backtracks at this. She thinks she touched the boy during their fight, but prolonged contact? There was none.

It wasn't her fault. Relief swept through her veins like a summer breeze. This wasn't her fault, he wasn't dying because of her. It didn't change the fact that he was still dying, but at least she knew it wasn't because of her.

That raised other questions, though. If she hadn't caused it, who had? The only logical answer was that there was another colorless somewhere on the Azura Isles. Someone else could drain the color from the unsuspecting people on campus and possibly the entire island.

They are in danger, if that is the case. But what can Dove do?

"Are there any other methods of infection that you

know of?" Dove asks. "Maybe proximity? Is contact a necessary part?"

The nurse scratches at her chin delicately, then shakes her head. "Not that our records indicate. Nearly every case of the Drain was spread through family members or life partners."

Then someone Lapis had prolonged contact with must have been the cause. Did he have a partner?

Guilt claws at her throat, scraping along the delicate skin beneath her necklaces. It wasn't her fault, but now there are more questions than answers. A prickle travels up her spine and into her hair. If it wasn't her, they were looking at a rogue colorless, one that had somehow escaped notice.

Dove stands and bows her head to the nurse. "Thank you. That's all the questions I have for now."

"Come back and visit if you think of more," the nurse replies before turning and disappearing around a corner.

Roan stands, his expression tight. Dove meets his gaze and the fear in her chest is overwhelming. Roan must see something in her expression; he reaches forward and takes her hands in his, squeezing gently.

"Dove," he says, softly, almost whispering. "It wasn't you."

She squeezes back. "I know. And that's what scares me."

13

———

CONTAGION

*D*ove stares at her reflection, tucking one strand of hair behind her ear. She isn't worried about her appearance, per se, but the task she's determined to accomplish today is difficult. She's stalling, and she knows it. But the thought of tracking down Lapis' friends is terrifying, and no amount of stalling will make the task less daunting.

Rory waits for her, twirling a curl of hair around her finger. Her lips are drawn tight—the most somber expression Dove has ever seen her wear.

Dove shakes her head at her reflection. She has to stop stalling.

"Good to go?" Rory asks, letting the curl fall loose from her finger.

Dove nods, a jerky movement that feels all wrong in her body, like someone else is controlling her. All she can think as she picks up her bag is of the last time she encountered these boys. Their accusatory stares and nasty words needle at her still, and she isn't so sure she can handle more of their abuse.

She will have Rory by her side, sure. But she doesn't

want Rory to hear those things, either. It's unpleasant having them directed at her—but it's infinitely worse having it directed at Rory.

Dove turns away from the mirror, her bag slung over one shoulder, and meets Rory's assessing gaze. The fabric of her dress swirls with her motion, brushing against her shins. Rory's gaze follows its sway.

The moment is over before Dove has time to process it, and Rory is across their room and opening the door for Dove, bowing dramatically. One corner of her mouth tugs up in that asymmetrical smile that makes Dove's heart race.

"After you, my lady," she says.

Dove curtseys. "Thank you, my lady." She is lighter on her feet than moments before.

Only Rory could do such a thing. She takes Dove's arm when they exit their dorm, looping her arm through and patting Dove's hand gently. They walk together, arm in arm, toward the Blue dorm on the other end of the small courtyard.

Cerise leaves and lapis flowers are in full bloom overhead, blue and red petals speckling the edges of Dove's vision as they walk. They occasionally dance in the light sea breeze, the sunlight filtering through them as they sway. Dappled patches of sunlight illuminate the stone walkway and gild Rory's dark hair.

Dove tightens their intertwined arms. Rory turns and flashes Dove that smile again, melting Dove's insides like the liquid gold that weaves through her hair. The feeling is indecipherable to Dove, but she likes it. It's preferable to the darker, squirming thing that knocks inside her brain, the twisting she's been ignoring as she walks with Rory.

The trip is short—too short, in Dove's opinion. The Blue dorm's flag flutters in the breeze and the cerulean hue is too dull and too bright all at once.

Inside, she greets the dorm manager with a polite nod. The manager smiles and waves them inside, the door's lock clicking open as they approach. They head for the common area. Rory's idea—and a good one at that. If they were to find Lapis' friends anywhere, it would be there.

The Blue dorm room is cozy, but elegant. Decorated in all hues of the house's namesake, its decor flows like the ocean. Tall, arching windows overlook an ornate rug and several seemingly random piles of squishy pillows, each bearing a student in their cradle. Couches line the edges of the rug and frame several bookshelves bursting with texts of all shapes and sizes. Several small circular tables intersperse themselves between the couches and students sit around their flickering oil lamps, working quietly on essays or playing chess.

When Dove steps inside, followed closely by Rory, her eyes drift around the expansive space. Several pairs of eyes lift to meet hers, although no one seems bothered by their sudden presence in a dorm that is obviously not theirs.

"So." An echoing, nasally voice quickly breaks the peace of the room. "The colorless is here to infect us all." A boy with hair the color of straw stands as he speaks. "Haven't you done enough?"

The calm of the common area breaks. It doesn't turn to a stampede, but the scrape of chairs on the floor and the stifled murmurs are somehow worse. Although the chancellor has done what she can regarding Dove's reputation, it is another thing to be accused of a crime no one understands.

The room empties quickly, leaving behind only the boy with the straw-colored hair and another whose face is screwed into a nasty snarl.

He speaks again, voice thick with contempt. "Here to finish what you started, colorless? As if taking Lapis' soul wasn't enough, now you want all of ours?"

Rory shoves past Dove, knocking their shoulders together. She advances on the boy, stomping over the piles of pillows and slamming her feet on the floor so hard it seems to shake the entire room.

Dove runs after her, catching her arm before she can reach him. "Rory, stop!"

Rory tries halfheartedly to pull her arm from Dove's grasp, but Dove knows she isn't using her full strength. Instead, she stares at the boy, face stormy. "She didn't give him the Drain, halfwit. Maybe if you'd actually asked the nurses about Lapis, you'd know that it couldn't have been her!"

The boy sneers at Rory. "Maybe if the school hadn't let her in, we wouldn't have to ask nurses about him!"

"Prism is open to everyone. Dove got in on her own merits, just the same as the rest of us. Are you questioning the chancellor's decisions?"

"Of course not, I'm questioning your sanity for sticking with her!"

"You little   "

Rory tries again to pull from Dove's grasp but she holds firm, interlocking her fingers in Rory's and squeezing as tightly as she can. "Stop, Rory. This will solve nothing! Please!"

"She's right," the boy says mockingly. "You can't do anything to me."

Rory goes red, a sharp color that matches the cerise blooms outside. Brilliant, fiery, and absolutely terrifying. Dove grips her hand tighter.

"Look," Dove tries, desperate to ask her questions and leave. "We just want to ask about Lapis so we can figure out how he got the Drain. Then we'll leave you alone. I want to be here even less than you want us to be."

The boy scoffs, and his friend echoes him. He crosses his arms over his chest defiantly and looks Dove in the eyes. "We all know how he got it. It was you."

Dove shakes her head, keeping her grip tight on Rory's hand. "The nurses said transference of the Drain requires prolonged contact. Which I didn't have with Lapis. Can you think of anyone, a partner, perhaps, that he might have had that sort of relationship or contact with?"

The boys both laugh, the echo loud and mocking. The boy with the straw hair doubles over and Rory finally stops struggling. Dove turns to look at her, fingers still intertwined. Rory's face has become a mask of calm. For some reason, that is more concerning to Dove than when she was furious.

Rory detangles their fingers, patting Dove's hand gently before stepping over a pile of pillows separating her from the boy. He straightens at her approach, wiping tears from his eyes. Before he can react, Rory grabs the front of his jacket and pulls his face close to hers.

"I know you want us gone," Rory says, voice dangerously low. "And we're more than happy to leave if you answer Dove's question." She shakes him, his head snapping back at the movement and startling him into silence. "Now."

The boy stares at Rory, tears still trickling from the corners of his eyes, but he is no longer smiling. He shakes his head slowly, trying to pull his face away from Rory's.

"Did he have any other friends, people he hung out with often? Other than you lot?"

The boy shakes his head again and brings both hands to Rory's wrists to loosen her grasp. She doesn't budge.

Rory stares down her nose at him. Dove thinks she

looks a bit like the chancellor that way, with all the same grace and poise she knows the woman possesses. But there's something deeper in Rory's expression, something visceral that doesn't mesh with the elegance Dove usually associates with her.

"Please." The boy's voice has gone high pitched and shaky. "We barely knew him. We met during the Revelation Ceremony—I don't know if he has other friends. He never mentioned them!"

Rory holds him for two more heartbeats, then lets him go, dropping him with a slight push toward the ground. The boy drops and lands on his backside with a muffled thump. When Rory turns to face Dove again, her face is still impassively calm.

"We're done here. Let's go."

Dove nods. Rory sweeps past her, curls bouncing as she strides toward the door. Before they leave the Blue common room behind, Dove looks back once more at the boy now standing from the floor.

He dusts his pants off and stares back at her, a frown creasing the space between his brows. He does nothing, only stares as Dove rounds the corner and he disappears from sight.

Rory flies through campus, her strides long. Dove has to run to keep up with her. She tries catching Rory's hand and misses, tries calling to her but to no avail. Rory keeps walking, past the dorms and into the quad, beyond the trees ringing the library and toward the small pond and the willow tree's long tendrils.

She parts the branches and tucks herself at the base of the tree. With a final thump, she loses all the frenetic energy that has been pouring from her in waves.

Dove follows her, gently pushing aside the branches of the willow tree to watch Rory lean her head back on the tree's thick trunk. She kneels beside Rory, her skirts billowing.

Dove reaches to take Rory's hand, but hesitates. Even if she didn't cause Lapis's Drain, there was still no proof that she *couldn't* cause the Drain in someone else. She can't be careless now—not when there is still so much at stake. There's a brief sense of relief that she knows what not to do. But the reality quickly crushes it that she still, no matter how much she wants to, touch Rory.

There is simply too much at risk.

Instead, she sighs. Rory's eyes are closed, but Dove knows she'll listen. "Thank you," Dove whispers. She knows it isn't enough, not to express what she's feeling. Not enough to truly embody everything Rory has done for her.

"What for?" Her eyes stay closed while she murmurs.

Dove settles in next to Rory, resting her head next to Rory's on the tree trunk. The bark is rough and scratchy through her hair, the ground hard beneath her. Their shoulders don't touch, but Dove can sense Rory, the same way she can sense the sun on her skin.

What is this feeling? The bubble in her chest is too big, cracking her ribs apart in the sweetest way, like her chest is made of spun sugar.

"For—" Dove begins, but cuts herself off. For everything, she wants to say, but that is not specific enough. For being Rory, she thinks, but that does not explain the real reason.

Rory turns her head, cracking one beautiful eye at

Dove. She smiles, crooked and perfect. "For kicking their asses?"

Dove giggles, the sound unanticipated. It barrels through her in a wave of unexpected joy. "For being there."

Rory's smile only grows. They stay there, gazes bearing into one another, neither wanting to be the first to look away. Dove breaks their eye contact first, her face inexplicably hot. Dove brings her hand to her face. The skin of her cheek is too warm, but so is her hand.

Rory turns away, her gaze landing on the quiet lake beside the willow tree. Its water is glass-like, reflecting fluffy white clouds and perfect cerulean sky. The picture it paints is a serene one, but it isn't enough to make the smile fading from Rory's face any less concerning.

She stays quiet, and Dove doesn't press. She isn't even sure what to ask.

Rory stares at the lake while her jaw flexes and unflexes. It's obvious something is bothering her. Dove can make several guesses as to what those things might be, considering the same doubts and anxieties are worming away at her heart as well.

If there really was no one else Lapis might have associated with, then how did he contract the Drain? Maybe this mysterious disease wasn't the Drain at all, but something much, much worse? If that was the case, then Dove and Roan's visit to the hospital may have been fruitless. And worse, it might have put both of them in danger.

Of course, it didn't matter much if Dove herself contracted the Drain. She had no color to begin with, so would the Drain even affect her? If there was nothing for her to lose, was she immune?

"Dove." Rory cuts through Dove's thoughts with a

soft voice. "I just—"

Rory leans over and grabs Dove's face between her hands. Her palms are soft, warmed from the sun and slightly damp from the ground. She smells like the earth. Dove's heart is slamming in her chest, almost painfully fast. It makes breathing a difficult affair.

Her cheeks are squished, so her words emerge muffled. "What's wrong?"

Rory lets go suddenly, jerking back as if burned. "I was"—she pauses, swallowing hard—"scared, for you. I just hate the way you're treated so callously. It's not fair."

Dove bites her lip. "Life is rarely fair."

"I *know* that," Rory continues. "But it doesn't change the fact I can't help but get angry on your behalf. What those boys said to you...it was *wrong*!"

Dove's heart lurches. For Rory to be so fired up on her behalf is both flattering and concerning all at once. Dove knows that what the boys said to her was unfair, but there was nothing she could do to change their minds. They'd made up their opinions of her, and although Dove's heart wanted her to fight, the logical part of her understood that it would simply be a waste of her energy.

Dove takes Rory's hand and interlocks their fingers. "You're right, Rory. But I can't—*we* can't change their minds, nor do I really want to try."

"But they're horrible!" Rory protests.

Dove nods. "Exactly. And that's why it's not worth it to try."

Rory is silent after this, her face screwed up in a half frown, half contemplative grimace. She doesn't let go of Dove's hand, but she turns to face the lake again.

Something in Dove twists. She hadn't realized just how she felt about the encounter until she talked through it with Rory. Her chest relaxes, unfurling like a contented, sunbathing cat. It's a pleasant realization, and Dove fortifies her resolve. She will get to the bottom of this. But to do so, she'll need Rory.

"I want to figure out how Lapis contracted the Drain," Dove says. "And I can't do it without your help."

Rory turns and squeezes Dove's hand. "I'm all yours, Dove."

14

———

HISTORY

The sun has just barely peeked its head over the horizon, its zenith long off. Dove hurries across campus alone toward the only place she might find answers.

The library is illuminated from behind by the rising sun, bathing it in gold and sparkling off the glass windows. The sight is comforting, somehow. The library has been a safe haven of sorts for Dove during her time on campus.

Her mission today is the same as before—she needs to know more about the colorless. Because she didn't spread the Drain to Lapis. She needs to know who, or what, *did*.

Inside her brown leather bag, she's kept the list from the librarian about the books she should seek for more information about the colorless. She didn't tell Rory where she was going, and the guilt nibbles gently at her insides as she pulls the doors to the library closed behind her. She knows Rory wants to help and she knows she *needs* Rory's help. But she has to figure out where to begin before she can ask. Otherwise, it's only a waste of her time.

The library is as welcoming as ever, the orange dawn

light illuminating the white marble floor to look like lava. Dove steps over them lightly, imagining herself walking across their molten pools like the magma birds of ancient tales. The librarian is not at his desk—in a way, Dove expects this. It's much too early for anyone to be here, precisely why she wanted to come this early.

She commandeers a spot at the first floor tables and sets down her bag with a thump. From inside, she pulls the list in the librarian's neat handwriting and finds the next title that is not crossed off.

Dove locates the book slowly, the clicking of her heels the only sound in the quiet library. It is rhythmic and cyclical, the rise and fall of each footstep echoing against the silent books. She drags a hand along the spines and revels in the leather's smell and dust.

Here, she is normal. Here, she can imagine herself as just another student researching her chosen discipline.

The book is nestled at the back of a stack, high enough up that Dove must stand on her toes to reach it. She stretches tall, shoulders straining as she reaches for the book, only for a shadow to eclipse her and grasp the book in her stead.

She jumps, falling against the shelf in a flurry of frantic movement. The hand holding the book lowers and chuckle sounds from behind her.

"Sorry," says Roan, "I didn't mean to scare you."

Dove presses a hand to her heart, trying to calm its furious thumping against her ribcage. "Colors! I didn't hear you at all," she breathes through the pounding blood in her veins.

Roan hands her the book wryly, meeting her eyes and cocking one dark eyebrow. A dry smile curves the corners of his lips. "You were very focused on the book." He turns the book sideways to glance at the cover. "More history research? Did you choose a concentration?"

Dove shakes her head and takes the book from Roan. "I'm still undeclared."

"Then why the research at dawn?" Roan asks, stepping away to allow Dove room to pass him.

She doesn't answer right away, turning to walk back to her table. She doesn't know why she's hesitating—something about revealing why she's here feels... incredibly personal.

Roan doesn't press, though. He simply follows, hands tucked into his trouser pockets. He looks even better than before, somehow. Lighter on his feet and like he's filled with color. His hair is more lustrous and his eyes seem to sparkle brighter. The dawn light favors him as they pass through more molten puddles of it.

"I'm researching the colorless," Dove finally says, although the words are heavy and thick in her mouth. "I know nothing about who I am. I want to know, I—*need* to know."

Roan's expression is unreadable; nothing is betrayed in his ocean eyes. But Dove swears he bristles. She watches him as they return to her table, watches the way his eyes graze over her bag and the list of books beside it. How they bounce down to the book she set on the table. How his gaze eventually returns to her, to her face. His expression is still a mystery when he finally speaks.

"You didn't do anything wrong, Dove," he says. "Don't let what those boys said to you get under your skin."

Dove smiles softly. "That's not why I'm doing this, you know."

Roan stares, face unchanged. "Then why?"

"I already told you," she says, face falling, "I need to know what, *who*, I am."

Roan's face finally changes. He frowns, the crease between his brows deep, like she has spoken in a language he doesn't understand. He chews his lip, then shifts uncomfortably from one foot to another.

Dove waits. She doesn't move, leaving the book between them on the table and her hands by her sides. Words bubble inside her, words that beg to burst free from her lips, words to explain more, to make Roan understand why she needs to do this.

She's never known who she is. She didn't know herself before the Revelation ceremony—she doesn't know anyone who did. A soul color gives your life context, gives your soul meaning. Without one…well, Dove doesn't feel like a person. She feels incomplete.

Knowing something, *anything*, about the colorless will be the first step to being whole. Toward understanding just who and what she is.

The desire to know herself is impossible to put into words without baring the deepest recesses of her empty soul to him. She isn't ready for that. She doesn't know if she'll ever be ready for that.

But it doesn't change her desire to know who she is.

Roan must sense something in her attitude, some subtle shift in her stance or a change in the way she carries herself. His face relaxes into a half-smile.

He shrugs. "Knowing yourself isn't something you can find in a book, Dove."

Dove knows he's right, but she has nowhere else to turn. There is no frame of reference for her, no one she can talk to who will understand. No one can help her untangle the knot that is the threads of her sense of self.

Even Rory, with her beautiful lopsided grin and sunshine personality, wouldn't ever be able to fully understand Dove, not when her soul was the rarest and most treasured.

"I—" She bites her lip. How does she explain? How can she put into words how terribly lonely it is to be so unknown?

Roan sighs, then pulls a chair out to sit. All tension is gone from his body, all strangeness has evaporated. When Dove looks at him, it's as if he never questioned her at all.

"You don't have to explain," he says, voice near a whisper. "I may not understand, but I can understand seeking solace anywhere you might find it."

Something else hovers around Roan now, something softer, something sadder. Something Dove doesn't understand. She sighs into the thought, melting into the irony of it all. She doesn't understand many things— herself is just the first entry on her list.

She sits too, laying a hand on the book. "I know it doesn't come from books. But where else can I go? I have no one to explain any of this to me."

Roan stares, his lips parting softly like he wants to reply but doesn't know how. Dove stares back, waiting, as the sun finally crests over the horizon and drenches the library in gold.

Their conversation ends there, a string not yet tied off, a broken thread left to dance in the wind. Roan stands and nods to Dove, and without saying another word, exits the library.

After Roan is gone, Dove returns to her book. She scans the pages hungrily, soaking in the history of the soul classes and hoping against all hope that there is a small nugget of knowledge that can help her.

What she finds is something she never expected.

The book describes the same things she already knows—the red, the blue, and the yellow feathers, all taken from the Goddess' tail, all breathed with the gift of life. All cherished as the Goddess' children. Her love, her devotion, and her sudden disappearance.

But she also finds the colorless. Upon the Goddess' vanishing, a new phenomenon swept through the Azura Isles: babies with no color were born to families across their small country, children whose loving touch would drain their parents and siblings of life. Children who never lived long past adolescence and would fade soon after their families did. Children who, in their early hours of life, were revealed to be colorless by the Aura Mirror.

Back then, the islanders blamed this phenomenon, this sickness, on the disappearance of the Goddess. And in some way, Dove supposed, they were probably right. The removal of her power inevitably caused something within the balance of their world to shift. Her departure caused a rift—a rift that was reflected in the souls of the children she so loved.

The book does not reveal much more from that period, but Dove can surmise what happened. The colorless died out, leaving only the descendants of those who'd been blessed by the Goddess. Since then, the colorless occasionally appear, and in their anomalous wake, a new wave of sickness.

Others have entered the library by now. The librarian has taken up residence behind his desk; other students shuffle to the surrounding tables, not one uttering a single word. Dove watches them, envies them for their indifference, for the ease in which they move through life as the beloved of the Goddess.

Dove slams the book shut. Inside her churns a thousand different emotions, all swirling and dancing too fast for her to isolate and name. Each one flits by her with the grace of a butterfly, only to fall beneath the shadow of another as quickly as it appears.

She is angry, one moment. Angry she is just one of these plagues that has appeared. Angry that, according to this, she has never been loved by the Goddess who disappeared.

She is hurt, the next. Hurt that, despite all her years of hoping, despite all the years of wishing, she is nothing more than a blight.

Then, the anger and hurt turns to confusion. It winds up her spine and curls around her shoulders, holding her eyes to the cover of the book.

Her family was never sick. If contact, prolonged contact, truly was the way to spread the Drain, how had her parents never fallen ill? Their family wasn't one that lacked physical affection; her parents hugged and kissed her all the time.

What kind of phenomenon is she? A colorless who doesn't spread the Drain?

It seems unlikely, nigh impossible. She's accidentally touched Rory plenty of times since they began living together and she is perfectly fine.

Dove doesn't know where this new information will lead her. She cannot fathom what comes next. Do the doctors know of her condition? Should she tell the chancellor? Maybe the Aegis Order needs to know.

Her only idea now is to go back to Hyacinth and Chancellor Brigaine. She's done enough on her own—she needs more if she is ever going to solve this. Dove knew she needed a path forward before she involves Rory in her plans, and now she has them.

Unease settles over Dove. She's at the edge of a cliff, teetering over the side into a new, undiscovered future. Everything will change; she is prepared for this, she thinks. After all, it's the reason she came to the library that morning. But the fear of the unknown is coalescing in her veins.

Rory's face swims into her vision. Her crooked smile and the lines that form around her cerulean eyes. Dove is lighter, because that's what Rory does for her.

She sighs and stands from the desk, just as the doors to the library open and light spills in.

Dove turns her eyes to the figure now enshrined in golden light, squinting against its glare, and finds a boy, hair as golden as the sun streaming behind him.

But there is something wrong. There are marks on his face, scratches that ooze bright red blood.

"Dove," Jasper wheezes. He's out of breath, chest heaving as if his next words will steal all the breath he has remaining. "Help. Me."

The last of his air is gone, and he collapses into a pool of sunlight, his hair streaked with gray.

15

———

UMBRA

*J*asper is taken away, just like Lapis, his color fading before Dove's swimming eyes.

She can't breathe as the car takes him away, rattling over the cobblestone paths and echoing in her ears. Dove knows she didn't do this, but the guilt eats at her, anyway. Why Jasper? Was she somehow the cause of all this, even if all evidence points to the Drain being spread by contact?

Her blood runs cold. She has had contact with Jasper—he caught her on the stairs just a few weeks ago. What if that was enough?

It still doesn't explain anything about her parents or the Valerus siblings, though. She's certainly had more contact with them than she ever had with Jasper.

What if the Drain could only be spread after discovering she has no soul color? What if her parents never got sick because until she knew she was colorless, it was simply impossible? The book had mentioned how they used to discover colors at birth—why that tradition changed, she doesn't know. But it would explain why the sickness only appeared after she discovered she was colorless.

150

Her stomach drops to her toes. If that's the case, then there are so many more people who might be sick, her parents included. She remembers the way they held her only a few short weeks ago at Parent's Day. If her theory is correct, then Rory is in danger. Roan, too.

Dove must remove herself from campus, from the island. It's the only way. There is simply too much at stake for her to continue the way she has been. She is putting everyone's lives in danger, and hurting those she cares most about. She can't continue to exist the way she has if she can hurt people she loves so easily.

Rory's crooked smile swims into her vision again, and she chokes back a sob.

The library is deadly quiet except for the sounds of her cries. No one has come near since the Order took Jasper away. Not even the librarian has approached her as she sits in the atrium, drenched in white-hot sunlight.

She stays there, dress pooling around her legs, and cries. She's alone—so incredibly alone. She can't do this by herself. But Goddess, it seems she must. The thought of a life spent entirely on her own sends more sobs wracking through her chest.

"Dove?" The voice is quiet as it calls her name, tender as a summer breeze.

Arms wrap around her shoulders and squeeze. Curls, soft and brown, rub against her tear-soaked cheeks. And Rory, all of her, fills Dove's senses. She holds Dove, burying her face in the crook of Dove's neck. Dove holds her back, twisting her fingers into the fabric of Rory's sweater. She melts into Rory, letting herself let go for just a moment.

But the fear sweeps in soon after, and Dove pushes Rory away with a sob. "You can't. I don't want you to get sick because of me."

Rory looks...colors, Dove doesn't know how to describe the look on Rory's face. It hovers somewhere between melancholy and anguish. Like Dove burned her when she pushed away. It breaks Dove's heart. She knows none of this is Rory's fault—Rory, the only person who's been steady through this entire ordeal. The person who's stood by her from the beginning.

Dove's vision swims again. "I'm sorry," she cries. "I'm sorry, I'm so sorry!"

Rory crosses the space between them in two long strides and gathers Dove in her arms again. One hand wraps around the back of Dove's head, Rory's long fingers weaving in her hair and cradling her. The other wraps beneath her arm and up her back, pressing her into Rory's chest.

"I'm sorry," Dove cries again into Rory's chest, her words muffled. Her hands stay in fists at her sides. She can't return the embrace—not without the fear of draining Rory of all her color.

Rory shushes Dove, stroking her hair gently. "You have nothing to apologize for, Dove."

"But—"

Rory clutches Dove tighter to her chest, stifling her attempt at protestation. "You have nothing to apologize for," she repeats, voice nearly a whisper.

Her chest is hollow, her heart beats too quickly, frantic and unable to settle. Everything is tight, too tight. If she tries to take a deep breath, her back spasms. Rory's grip is tight but not constricting. But Dove still can't draw a full breath. Her blood feels like it's on fire, burning all her veins away while her heart turns to ash.

But the longer they stay like this, the slower its beat goes. Her blood cools, her veins aren't fit to burst. She feels...better than she's felt in a long time. Something in her is healing, something she didn't know was broken.

Her hands come to Rory's back of their own accord, knotting once more in her sweater, another tangling in her curls.

Rory pulls back, just a little, to meet Dove's gaze. Her dusk-colored eyes quiver.

Dove releases Rory, but Rory doesn't do the same. Her hands move to either side of Dove's face, grasping her cheeks between her soft palms. A thumb strokes the curve of Dove's jaw. Neither says a word—they stay there, saturated in sunlight in the doorway to the Prism Library, and the world drops away. There is nothing left in Dove's eyes but Rory.

That feeling she's been avoiding, the one that hovers in her chest, crashes up through her and threatens to spill out her mouth. She doesn't know what it will mean when it does, but she tries so hard to stop it. She's unsuccessful.

"I..." Dove begins, unable to stop herself. "I don't want to hurt you, Rory."

That takes her by surprise. It's accurate, of course, but it's not what she expected to say. Dove was sure she was about to admit...

Admit what?

Rory's shoulders soften; her thumb traces the apple of Dove's cheek and wipes the tears away. "You haven't, you aren't, and I don't think you will."

Dove shudders. "Not on purpose. But I'm colorless— it's dangerous for you to be around me."

"I don't care," Rory says. "You're my..."

Rory stops abruptly, biting her lip in a show of hesitation Dove has never seen from her before. It's surprising and strange, an expression she would never associate with Rory.

Dove tries to fill in the space Rory left. "Friend?"

Rory stiffens, then shakes her head. "You're more than that. More than just a friend or a roommate."

This isn't happening. She can't. There are too many reasons not to get involved in this. Dove doesn't want to hurt Rory with the Drain. She doesn't want to cause her pain.

"I—" Dove begins, forcing the words out through a mouth that feels full of sand, "I can't. I can't do this to you. It's forbidden."

Rory's tension leaks away and she releases Dove's face. "I know. I know it is and that's why I've been avoiding this for so long. But Dove...I can't lie to myself or to you any longer." She steps back, lowering her eyes to the ground. "But I understand if you don't want to be around me any longer. I understand if you hate me. But—I can't deny what I feel for you anymore."

Dove watches her stare at the ground, her chest deflating. "I don't hate you. How could I?"

The hope that shines in Rory's eyes breaks Dove's heart. In a perfect world, there would be no issue. Dove and Rory could be happy. But Dove is colorless, and she will hurt Rory—that is an inevitability.

"But I will hurt you if you stay by me. I'll hurt you if you hold me or kiss me. I can't do that to you." Dove exhales, releasing all the pressure that has built in her chest. With that loosening, the door of possibility closes. This can never be, no matter how badly she wants it to.

Rory nods. "I know. Even so, it doesn't change how I feel."

Dove melts. Goddess, how she wishes things could be different. How she wishes she could hold Rory, stroke her curls, bury her face in her neck. But she knows it can't be—she cares about Rory too much to destroy her for a moment of bliss.

They both sigh, and whatever was between them is gone now. Dove clenches her fists and shakes her head. They've spent too long in proximity to each other. Time is of the essence. She needs to take Rory to the Aegis Order.

"Rory," she begins, and gestures for the other girl to follow her. "We need to go to see Hyacinth."

"Why?" Rory asks, cocking her head.

Dove pulls her bag further up her shoulder and starts walking down the stairs. "Because you may be infected."

The Aegis Order's headquarters are in the center of the city. Street cars crisscross the cobblestone streets and cerise trees provide shade beneath their crimson blooms. Although it is now midmorning, the streets are packed with people. Several young children dressed in the academy uniform of the Ceruleus school dart in front of Dove as she walks. A woman, only a few years older than Dove, runs after them, scolding. Two men in flowing robes walk just ahead, the lettering on their shoulders designating them as city officials. People jump from the street cars and walk briskly to their destinations, colors and fabrics of all kinds flashing in and out of Dove's vision so quickly she may faint from the stimulation.

Rory, however, is unperturbed. She grew up here, in the bustle of Ceruleus, so it is only natural she knows how to navigate it properly. Dove focuses on her curls as they bounce ahead of her. She's afraid if she takes her attention off Rory for even one moment, she will lose her in the crowd.

But the other, more visceral fear, is that every brush

of a stranger's shoulders and every touch of someone's body against her own in this crowd is another infection, another Drain she cannot stop. It eats at her each time she feels another connection. The tension is so heavy, Dove fears she will snap beneath its weight.

Their journey ends before a tall, peach-colored building crisscrossed in dark wood accents. Scalloping lines the roofline in a welcoming, homey sort of way, and a sign designating this as the Aegis Order headquarters sways in the breeze. Dove doesn't relax.

Rory pushes ahead, opening the dark wooden door for Dove and gesturing her inside.

The headquarters are a welcome reprieve from the bustle of Ceruleus, quiet and dark to the city's bright noise. It's a vacuum here—the air is still and cool on Dove's sticky skin. She welcomes its embrace with an internal sigh.

Rory stands watch at her side as they take in the space. The ceiling is tall, reaching high enough to expose a balcony to a second floor where several people in the dark blue uniforms of the Aegis Order bustle back and forth. Here on the first floor, only a few people mill about, most not in uniform. Other visitors, Dove assumes.

A guard (Dove recognizes his uniform from when they visited the campus and Chancellor Brigaine several months ago) approaches them with long strides. He is tall, dark-haired, and wears a pair of dark round glasses, even though they are inside.

He speaks roughly when he approaches. "State your business."

Rory looks him up and then down again, steel in her spine. "We need to see Hyacinth. It's about the Drain."

The guard regards Rory with what Dove thinks might be contempt, but it's hard to tell behind his glasses. He nods curtly and gestures to a bench in an alcove along a wall. "Wait here."

Dove obeys, but Rory stays standing, crossing her arms in a pose that makes her look ten times taller than she actually is. The scowl is the last touch needed to tie the facade together. But Dove knows better, and something in her heart roils at how Rory is standing guard. For her.

The guard is slow. They wait for over ten minutes for him to return, a briskly walking Hyacinth in tow. When she spots Dove, her grim expression turns soft.

"Dove?" she says when she reaches them. She gestures to the guard to leave, and he obeys with a small dip of his head. "Come, let's talk in my office."

They follow Hyacinth to a wooden staircase on the other side of the large reception space and head upstairs. Dove's shoes clack too loudly on the wood, a repetitive *thwack* in her mind that does nothing to still her racing thoughts.

She is afraid, if she is honest with herself. She is terrified of the future, what it may look like, if her theory is true. If she can spread the Drain as easily as a simple touch, then there is no hope for her for a normal future. Even Hyacinth, who has been nothing but truthful and kind to Dove, will deny that her presence in society is dangerous.

Her heartbeat is loud in her ears as they reach the second floor. Rory glances at Dove from the corner of her eyes. She must see something on Dove's face—Rory has reached down and grabbed her hand. She gives it a gentle squeeze, but Dove tugs her hand away with a small shake of her head.

Hyacinth turns down a series of marble and wood hallways, then stops before a nondescript door with a golden plaque. She doesn't turn to see if the girls are following before pushing open the door and heading inside.

Her office is plain, unadorned with items of a personal nature. A neat desk stands in the center of the room, a comfortable chair pushed in and two armchairs turned slightly inward on the opposite side. Several bookcases line the walls, filled with file boxes, books, and stacks of paper. A small window overlooks the city center.

Hyacinth heads to her chair and sits heavily in it before gesturing to the chairs before the desk with a graceful wave of her hand. Dove and Rory both sit, but Dove perches on the end of her seat, ready to spring to her feet at any moment.

Hyacinth briefly turns her gaze to Dove, a wrinkle forming between her brows. She says nothing though and folds her hands in front of her and sighs.

"Emerald mentioned the Drain? What happened?"

Dove looks at Rory first, but when Rory opens her mouth, Dove speaks first. This is her issue, her problem to solve. Rory shouldn't have to do all the work for her.

"There was another case of the Drain on campus this morning," Dove says, her words coming in a deluge. They fall so quickly from her lips she mixes a few of the words together.

Rory raises her eyebrows and a small smirk spreads across her lips. Something shines in her eyes—pride, maybe? Dove doesn't know.

Hyacinth frowns, puckering her dark painted lips. "I just received the report from the hospital. What happened?"

"It was—" Dove begins, then stops short when an unexpected lump forms in her throat. Rory reaches over to place a hand atop hers, her warmth and strength flowing into Dove as she squeezes gently.

Dove heaves a lung-straining breath, then huffs it out

in a burst before beginning again. "A boy, one I'd talked with a few times before. He fell ill right before me."

The wrinkle between Hyacinth's brows deepens, but before she can speak, Dove keeps going. The words come faster now, everything that's been building inside of her coming out of her in a tidal wave.

"I know the hospital said that the Drain requires extended or frequent periods of touch, but what if I'm different somehow? What if I've infected everyone around me?" She shudders, unable to stop the sensation that travels up her spine. "I need to be isolated. Until they can figure out what actually causes the Drain."

Rory whips her head to Dove. "I thought we were coming to test me, not lock you away!"

Dove shakes her head. "I'm a danger to society, a danger to you and to everyone on campus and this island. I can't—I can't stay here any longer if I'm going to keep infecting others."

"You know that's not true! I'm perfectly fine—no fading in sight! I've been around you longer than either Lapis or Jasper was. If you really were a danger, wouldn't I have faded long before Jasper did?" Rory shoots up from her seat. She's practically screaming, her voice a pitch higher than Dove has ever heard it. "And Roan! Roan has been around you as much as I have and he's totally fine too! There must be something else going on, some other condition, but it's not you, Dove. We already discovered that you didn't infect Lapis, didn't we?"

Hyacinth watches Rory's speech with a practiced indifference, the type of face Dove thinks she must make when listening to petitions or defenses. A face that gives nothing of what the woman wearing it is thinking. Hyacinth holds up a delicate hand and gestures for Rory to sit back down. Rory doesn't obey.

"Dove," Hyacinth begins, her voice even and low, "I need more information. I appreciate your concern for others here, and I agree the risk is simply too great." She sighs, a deep, heavy thing that seems to melt all the weight from her body. "I'd like to propose that you quarantine at the hospital. We'll have the doctors run some tests on you. We are woefully under-prepared and uneducated on the conditions that spread the Drain—we only have historical texts from hundreds of years ago, and they did not have the technology we have now."

Dove nods. "Thank you, Hyacinth. I think this is the only right path forward."

"In addition," she continues, turning her steely gaze to Rory, "I would like to test all those you've had prolonged contact with. Rory, report to the hospital with Dove as well. If you have shown no symptoms yet, it doesn't mean you are safe. I'll be reporting there myself, as well as the chancellor, once we contact your parents." She stands, pushing up from her chair. "Is there anyone else we should test?"

Dove looks at Rory and worry bubbles in her chest. "Roan. And the librarian from the Academy."

Hyacinth nods. "Very well. There's no time to waste— I'll gather the rest of these individuals. Please head to the hospital immediately, girls."

With her chest encased in iron, Dove stands from her chair and bows her head to Hyacinth in thanks. Finally, she might have answers. But the tightness in her chest is too heavy. If she really causes the Drain, if she really condemned Jasper and Lapis to this terrible fate, she doesn't know what she will do.

And if Rory is infected…

Then she will have no choice but to run to the sea, never to return.

16

LUCENT

*D*ove is sure of herself. Her spine is straight, her heart calm as she walks into the hospital once more and flags down the nearest staff member. Her voice does not shake when she explains what Hyacinth sent her here to do. She does not tremble when the nurse takes her to a quiet wing in the hospital after donning a face mask.

And she most certainly does not cry when the door to a blank room shuts behind her.

No, she only allows herself to collapse when the nurse is most definitely gone, with promises to return later after Hyacinth has gathered those that may be infected and briefing them.

Her tears are hot and fat, burning her skin as they fall. She is well and truly alone now, quarantined in a tiny, white room. She is doing this to herself and she doesn't regret her choices. But she cannot stop her hands from shaking.

There is a small window that offers reprieve, its view a top-down of the Ceruleus city center and the sparkling azure ocean beyond. The dawn finally has broken into a glorious day and the waves sparkle like the sea glass Rory gave her so long ago. Colorless, but sparkling. Beautiful in its own way.

Something inside of Dove shifts. She's been driven along by the tides of fate until now. But today she made a choice—a choice where she is putting her fate in her own hands. From now on, she will be the charioteer of her own destiny. Even if that destiny means leaving everything and everyone she loves behind.

She swipes at the tears still lingering on her cheeks with the back of her hand. Her fate is hers—she's done moping and feeling sorry for herself. She's done plenty of that since her Revelation Ceremony. It will not help her to continue, not when so much hinges on her, now.

Dove taps both cheeks with her hands and turns from the window. The door to her room opens, and the nurse, Hyacinth, the chancellor, and Rory greet her.

Her stomach drops. Why are they here? If she is truly contagious, if she is dangerous in any capacity, having them here is madness. She opens her mouth to argue, but before she can, Hyacinth smiles.

"We're unaffected, Dove," she says, and Chancellor Brigaine nods with her. "The doctors ran a few tests and we are fine. Just fine."

The relief is both light and so, so heavy. She thinks maybe she can fly. She thinks maybe she could sink to the bottom of the ocean. Both sensations live in her chest and fight a war with each other but she doesn't care. They're *fine*. They're *safe*.

Which means, no matter what, she isn't the reason Jasper or Lapis got sick.

Rory runs to Dove and wraps her in a deep, unyielding embrace. Dove doesn't hesitate to return it. Dove buries her face in Rory's neck, inhaling her scent and relishing her warmth.

The nurse is smiling when Dove and Rory break their embrace. "We're still running tests on your family and the other individuals Hyacinth brought in, but we are confident they will also receive a clean bill of health."

Dove nods her head. "Thank you. I'm..." She trails off, unable to say just what she is feeling. She's never felt relief like this before, and it is more than just simply challenging to describe. It's impossible to put into words.

Rory squeezes her hand, their fingers interlocked. "Can we see Jasper?"

The nurse nods. "That would be acceptable. Please follow me."

Hyacinth and the chancellor follow the nurse while Dove and Rory trail behind, fingers still interlocked. The waves in her stomach are back—she doesn't know how she can face Jasper. He is so colorful in her memories. And although she is not the cause of his condition, she doesn't want to tarnish the joyful person in her memories.

But she needs to face this. She needs to see him, no matter how much she wants to cling to the person she thought she knew.

They arrive before a closed wooden door, and the nurse gestures for them to wait. She enters first, murmuring a few soft words and adjusting the curtain around the bed. When she is finished, she gestures for them to enter. Hyacinth steps forward, but the chancellor hangs back.

"I'll give you three some time before I return." The nurse's smile doesn't reach her eyes. "His parents will be here soon."

The sadness turns sharp in Dove's belly—she can't imagine the agony of seeing your child this way. Although she knows she is not the cause, the thought eats at her. It is not pity she feels, but a deep sort of loss she can't quite pinpoint.

Jasper is tucked beneath white hospital sheets, his eyes closed. He hasn't lost all of his color just yet, but his hair is streaked with white, and his normally golden skin is pale. From far away, he looks peaceful. But when Dove approaches his bedside, a small furrow between his brows tells her otherwise. His hands rest atop the sheets in loose fists. That, she supposes, is a good sign.

She takes one of his hands in her own and closes her eyes. Even though the Goddess is gone, maybe she can pray. Maybe she can beg whatever remnants might still live on this island for his recovery.

Footsteps echo on the hard floor. She cracks her eyes open to see Rory taking Jasper's other hand, just like Dove. Warmth tickles behind Dove's eyes. Rory hardly knows Jasper, barely ever interacted with him. But she is here, and Dove's heart is suddenly too big for her chest.

Rory nods to Dove, then closes her eyes. Together, they pray to the Goddess for Jasper's health.

Warmth courses through her. It burbles up from deep in her belly, then spreads long fingers through her chest and head, until finally traveling down her arms and through her fingers. It doesn't burn. It's like a sunny summer day, pleasant and warm on her skin.

She breathes, in, then out, over and over. It becomes a sort of meditation, a trance. In for three, hold for five, out for seven. She never opens her eyes.

Goddess, she begs, Jasper doesn't deserve any of this.

The warmth spreads faster now, speeding down her arms and pouring from her fingertips. She doesn't know where it goes when it leaves her. Jasper's hand is weak in hers—no strength to grip her back, but she doesn't mind.

But then, there *is* strength. Suddenly, Jasper's hand tightens around hers.

Dove's eyes fly open to meet Jasper's alert gaze on hers. His eyes are bright, ringed in gold with gray at their center. But that gray is fading, just like the streaks in his hair are turning back to their burnished gold.

Rory is still gripping his hand, but her eyes are open too. They are wide and surprised as she stares down at Jasper, his color returning like ink spreading on a wet page. His skin darkens, his hair gilds.

Hyacinth gasps. "What the—"

The door to the room opens, and the chancellor steps in, two others in tow who look like they have stepped from a bath of gold. When they see Jasper, awake, alert, and regaining his color, they rush to his side.

The chancellor looks to Hyacinth, one eyebrow raised. "Hyacinth?"

Hyacinth shakes her head. "I have no idea."

Jasper's parents, full of tears and exclamations, come to take over where Rory and Dove were holding his hands. Dove moves aside, allowing one of Jasper's parents to take her place. The other parent stares down at their son and turns to Dove, an expression on their face that Dove cannot read.

"What happened? They told us he had the Drain, but he looks fine."

Dove shakes her head. "I don't know. Rory and I were just praying for him and then he..." She gestures to the bed where Jasper is now trying to sit up. His parent helps him to sit, supporting his back as he scoots up the bed.

Jasper's eyes meet Dove's. They are golden once more, full of life and color where they were blank and gray. She wouldn't have believed he ever had the Drain if she hadn't seen it for herself only moments before.

Hyacinth is staring, her eyes fixated on Jasper, surrounded by his parents and looking healthy, whole, and golden as the sun. Then she turns to Dove and gestures for her to follow.

Rory follows too, and they leave Jasper's room behind. Hyacinth seems distressed, her eyebrows pinched and lips pursed. She whirls on Dove after the door closes behind them.

"You're *sure* you saw him Drained this morning?"

Dove nods. "I know what it looks like, Hyacinth. He was most definitely Drained—I don't know what happened just now."

Hyacinth squints at Rory. "Did you see him this morning too?"

"No, but I believe Dove. You saw him when we first came in, didn't you?" Rory gestures back to the door. "He was most definitely Drained. Dove isn't lying."

Hyacinth sighs, rubbing her forehead. Footsteps echo from the opposite end of the hallway, and the Academy librarian and Dove's parents approach.

Dove doesn't wait for Hyacinth to continue; she sprints to her mother and father, arms open wide. They stop and open their arms in response, folding her into a tangled, messy embrace. They are so comforting, and the tears prickle her eyes again as she takes in their warmth.

"I'm so sorry," she says, hiccupping into her mother's shoulder. "I was so afraid I'd hurt you."

"We're fine, Dovey," her father replies, then kisses the top of her hair. "You have nothing to apologize for."

Dove pulls away—too soon, in her opinion—and faces Hyacinth once more. She doesn't understand what has happened here. First, everyone she's had contact with is fine, no Drain to speak of. Second, Jasper has made a miraculous recovery after holding her hand. Third, Lapis is still sick, and they don't know who is spreading the Drain.

Lapis. Dove gasps. "Hyacinth!" She yells, breaking from her parents' grasp and running back to the other woman. "I don't know how Jasper healed, but I think it has something to do with me." She stands up taller, straightening her spine. "If you agree, I think I would like to try healing Lapis, too."

Hyacinth does not reply right away. She instead stares at Dove, her face unreadable. Dove knows she's asking a lot. They have only just discovered she doesn't spread the Drain, but the fear is still there. Centuries of fear of the colorless is not so easily erased, and although Hyacinth has been kind, she is not reckless.

But there is no denying that Jasper has healed. His color has returned. If she can do the same for Lapis, she must try.

Hyacinth seems to recognize the determination in Dove's stance, the fire in her eyes. She sighs deeply, then nods. "It can't hurt to try, I suppose."

She retrieves the nurse and asks to have them escorted to Lapis' room. Dove's parents do not stay; they bid her a heartfelt farewell and promise to visit again soon. The librarian, however, asks to come along. Professional curiosity, he calls it.

In Lapis' room, the curtains are drawn and he lies perfectly still on his bed. He is so, so pale, even more so than the last time Dove was here.

She steps to his bedside, staring down at his pale fingers. If this doesn't work, she isn't sure what she will do. Dove breathes slowly, in and out, then grasps Lapis' cold fingers in her own. They are jarringly cold, like small blocks of ice.

Dove closes her eyes and prays. *Goddess, please heal him. Please.*

She waits, waits for the warmth to return. But it doesn't. She cracks an eye open, watching Lapis as he lays still in the bed, white as death. His color doesn't return.

Hyacinth lays a hand on her shoulder. "It's okay, Dove. You tried."

Dove doesn't move, still gripping Lapis' hand in her own. She hasn't tried hard enough. There must be something she is missing, something she isn't doing right.

"The window," she croaks. Her voice is so rough. "Open the curtains, please."

Rory obeys, and the light spilling in only illuminates just how pale Lapis truly is. Dove swallows, her throat like sandpaper. But she will try again.

Goddess, please heal him. Hear my pleas.

Nothing. His hands are freezing, his eyes closed and still beneath the thin skin of his lids.

What was she doing wrong? Why wasn't this working?

She thinks of how she prayed over Jasper, what was different. The realization hits her, but gently, like a petal on her hand. *Rory.*

"Rory," she gasps, eyes wide. "Take his other hand. Pray with me."

Rory looks confused but obeys. She takes Lapis' other hand and flinches at the cold but doesn't let go. She closes her eyes, both hands closed over the pale boy's.

This time, when Dove makes her plea again, something has changed. The warmth is there, budding deep in her belly and curling up through her chest, just like before. It travels down her arms, sluices through her veins. Until finally it reaches her fingertips and Lapis' hands begin to warm.

The cold melts from him. It happens slowly, like the sun shining on a glacier. But his hand thaws, curling in on itself as warmth returns in a crawl. Dove does not open her eyes; she stays with them firmly squeezed shut, praying and urging that warmth down her limbs harder with every passing moment.

It may not be her fault that Lapis fell ill, but if she can heal him, maybe this squirming in her heart will go away.

Finally, his fingers close around hers with his own strength. Dove opens her eyes to meet Lapis' sky blue eyes, no trace of white left.

"What..." he croaks, voice like rough bark, "happened?"

Dove tries to let go, but he grips tighter, awareness flooding into his veins with every passing second. He is more alert, his eyes bright.

He swallows heavily, then tries again. "What happened? What are you doing here?"

Rory drops his hand, flinging it back to the bed with little pomp. "We healed you. At least try to act grateful."

Lapis shakes his head. "No, that's not what I mean." He grips Dove's hand even tighter and tries to pull her closer. "I was fine, then nothing, then I woke up here. *What did you do to me?*"

Hyacinth steps beside Dove and pries Lapis' fingers from Dove's hand. The blood surges back into her veins, an unpleasant prickling sensation that she tries to alleviate by massaging her hand.

Hyacinth now stands over Lapis, arms crossed. "You were attacked by a colorless—not Dove, before you start throwing around accusations. In fact, Dove and Rory just healed you."

Lapis frowns, his jaw working frantically as he stares at his hands. He's avoiding meeting Hyacinth's eyes. She knows it. She leans down so she can see Lapis' face. Her expression softens and she uncrosses her arms.

"Lapis," she continues, her tone softer than it was before, "I know this must be confusing. We'll leave you in peace. But please, if you can remember anything, tell us who might have attacked you, that would be helpful."

Lapis turns his head from Hyacinth and says nothing. He looks awful, even with his color returned. His cheeks are sunken, his hair greasy. The hospital has been caring for him, but there's only so much one can do for someone who cannot eat, sleep, or care for themselves.

Dove steps away, heading for the door. She doesn't want to be here any longer—Lapis might be healed, but he still hates her. She will not subject herself to his vitriol when she has a choice.

Rory follows, just like Dove knew she would. Loyal, stubborn, beautiful Rory. The girl she could have if she wanted. The girl who would give her everything if Dove would just let her.

She steps outside and Rory closes the door after her. Silence prevails, but it is not an uncomfortable one. They listen to the soft murmurings of Hyacinth and Lapis in the room, unable to discern specific words. Dove doesn't mind—Lapis is healed, and what happens after is none of her concern. Guilt flares in her stomach at that, but she bites back. It truly isn't any of her concern what Lapis decides to do with his life. He is his own person and he will make his own choices. Choices she has absolutely no sway in. And she is satisfied with that.

"Dove?" Rory's voice cuts through her determination. "What did we do?"

Dove's been so caught up in the fact she *isn't* the cause of the Drain that she hasn't stopped to consider what she might be instead. Is she still colorless? Or is she something yet unknown, something yet untested, untried? Are the colorless really the cause of the Drain, or were the history books wrong?

Rory's fingers weave between her own. Her heart calms. This is how it always is with Rory—just one simple touch, one word from this beautiful girl, and she is whole.

She bites her lip, then sighs. "I don't know," Dove replies honestly. "I don't understand anything anymore."

Rory opens her mouth to reply, but footsteps interrupt her before she can. The librarian, the kind old man with twinkling eyes, rounds the corner and smiles when he spots them.

He settles into a chair along the wall before turning his gaze on Dove. "Perhaps I can help with that."

17

———

LUX

$\mathcal{D}$ove doesn't know how they got here.

She has returned to the library with Rory, after ensuring Hyacinth no longer needed them and that Dove's parents were indeed well. The librarian accompanied them all the way back and refused to answer any of their questions, simply citing that "they would understand soon."

He stays mysterious, but Dove does not fear something sinister. Curiosity is all that permeates the air as they stand before the desk. The librarian pulls a key from around his neck—it's an antique, brassy and worn to gold in some places. He uses it to open that shimmering gold lock she saw long ago on the rattan cabinet.

Whatever is inside must be important. But Dove doesn't understand what it has to do with *her*.

Inside rests a book. Because of *course* it's a book. This is a library, and the librarian is the one with the key. But the book is obviously old, judging by the curling, faded script on the cover. It is inlaid with gold and streaked with the primaries—Red, Blue, and Yellow—across its cover and spine.

The title reads, *Azura.*

The librarian lifts the book from the display case with great care, cradling the book as if it were a human babe. He brings it to his desk and places it atop the wood, face-up. Dove looks down at it, the title in broad blue strokes staring up at her like a beacon.

"Dove," the librarian says. He runs a hand gently over the front of the book, briefly blocking her view of the title. It's enough to break her trance. She glances up again to meet his deep purple eyes. "This book is very special. Do you know why?"

She shakes her head. Obviously it must be extraordinary, otherwise, why would it be under lock and key?

The librarian smiles. "It's the Goddess' book. A complete and true history of the islands, and what happened to her when she disappeared."

A gasp. Rory has her hands over her mouth, the sound having escaped her lips involuntarily. The frisson travels up the length of Dove's spine and coalesces at the base of her skull.

Dove swallows. "What do you mean? Why are you showing this to me? To us?"

His smile grows wider. "You'll understand once you read."

Neither girl moves. They stare at the librarian with open mouths and wide eyes, but he simply continues to smile while resting a hand on the book. Dove's heart is so loud in her ears she swears the librarian must be able to hear it.

"Go ahead," he says.

So Dove steps forward. Inside are the answers she's waited for all this time, the answers that poke and prod and tug at her insides. She'll finally understand who she is, *what* she is. Her hands shake as she reaches for the cover.

The librarian moves his wrinkled fingers and pushes it across his desk toward her.

The book is warm—a sensation that sends chills up Dove's spine. It is like a living thing. The cover is heavy, the pages yellowed but not brittle. A title on the inside is too faded for Dove to make out, but the letters don't look like the ones she knows.

She turns another page and her stomach performs an impressive series of acrobatics she wasn't aware was possible. This page is less faded than the original. It simply reads, *The Beginning.*

She flips one more time and senses Rory beside her. The warmth radiates from her like the sun; it's calming and comforting here in the dry cool of the library. Gooseflesh worms up Dove's bare arms as she begins to read.

In the beginning, there was only the Goddess. The Goddess created the oceans and the sky, splitting them down the middle and painting them blue so they would always reflect one another. Then she created the islands by cutting a lock of her hair and dropping it into the ocean. From its depths rose the land.

When the land solidified, the Goddess created the stars and the moon and gave the moon its sibling in the sun. She finally wiped her brow of sweat and created animals from the drops that fell to the islands.

But the Goddess was lonely. The birds would sing to her, and the otters would perform for her, but the animals could not talk to her. So, from her beautiful tail, she plucked a single red feather.

From it, she created her Steward and named him Aurus.

Aurus accompanied the Goddess across the ocean while she observed her creation. He would create stories of great waves in the ocean and water that fell from the sky, of hours where the sky turned purple and yellow and pink and hours when the moon would cast a white glow on the islands she created.

The Goddess loved the Steward's tales so much she made them real. She painted the sunsets with the feathers of her tail and wove moonlight from the trails left by falling stars. She created clouds that would deliver rain to the islands and asked the moon to move the ocean for her.

Because of his tales, the Steward helped the Goddess create an even more beautiful, rich, and colorful world than one she'd ever imagined.

The Goddess saw that the Steward was lonely; while he told her tales and spun magic with his words, she could not do the same for him. She was a goddess, and he was her creation. But because she loved Aurus, she wanted to give him a gift. Life that could be his own companion. Life that, if he desired, could inhabit this beautiful world he'd helped her create.

So, she plucked two more feathers from her tail.

The yellow feather became the Scholar, named

Lustro.

The blue feather became the Healer, named Caerulum.

Aurus, Lustro, and Caerulum lived on the islands for many years. The Goddess doted upon them, giving them everything they could ever desire. She would often walk the shores with them and share meals with them.

One day, after many years, Caerulum bore Lustro's child—the first child of the islands. In honor of their creator, they named the child Iris. Aurus and the Goddess loved the child as their own too, and she grew up knowing nothing but joy.

The Goddess granted Iris a mirror—one that would show her the color that her soul had taken. When she'd grown tall enough to stand on her own, Iris looked into the mirror and was pleased to see her soul shone with the deepest blue hue, just like the ocean the Goddess had created.

When Iris reached maturity, the goddess took her under her wing, teaching her magic to help the islands thrive. Iris was talented and created many beautiful things with the Goddess' teaching. She created colorful birds in the Goddess' image; she created fish that shone with the wonderful colors of her family.

Iris was talented; no one denied her this. They encouraged her creativity and allowed her to thrive. But with unbridled creativity and free rein eventually came hubris.

She was warned. Use too much power at once and lose everything that gave her life color. Because, as the goddess explained, the colors she had given Aurus, Lustro, and Caerulum were their souls, their life force. As their child, Iris was no different.

But Iris was young. She was sure of herself. And she overexerted her power when she tried to create her most ambitious creation to date: a lizard with great wings and a mane of fire.

It drained her and left her without color.

Distraught, the Goddess and her children did all they could to help Iris, but it was no use. She faded into dust. Upon her demise, the Goddess could no longer bear the guilt of teaching Iris the magic that eventually corrupted her.

Aurus did all he could to comfort their Goddess, but it was no use. She fell into a deep despair. The sun turned gray, and the rain fell for days. Nothing Lustro and Caerulum did could bring her back from the darkness. And eventually, the Goddess faded. Her soul cleft in two: one piece fell into the depths of the ocean, the other drifted into the sky on a shaft of sunlight.

The Steward, the Scholar, and the Healer knew they must continue the Goddess' legacy, knew they must continue the work she'd started and loved so deeply.

More children were born; more souls were colored in the Goddess' hues. Although her soul had cleaved, she was still present in each new life that came to be on the islands. Each child would gaze at the colors of their souls in the mirror, and each was taught that their color was the most precious gift from their Goddess.

Magic was forbidden—the fate that had befallen Iris could never happen again. And so Aurus, Lustro, and Caerulum took that knowledge to their graves.

When they did eventually pass, their souls became one with their children, and their consciousness lived on through the centuries. Although the memories would not always awaken each life, they would appear when they were needed.

And the original three never stopped searching for a way to reunite the cleaved halves of the soul of their precious Goddess.

Dove lifts her eyes to the librarian, who is watching with rapt attention. She doesn't understand. There are too many questions, too many moving pieces for her to sort into a clear picture she can easily understand.

But Rory doesn't hesitate.

"You," she says, voice quiet but powerful. Dove can only see her from the corner of her vision, her curly hair covering her eyes. "You're one of the three, aren't you?"

The librarian nods. "I am Aurus, yes."

"The Steward," Dove supplies. She frowns, glancing back down at the open book before her. "But I still don't understand—what does that have to do with us? With the colorless?"

The librarian smiles. "Come now, Dove, you're smarter than that. Think about it. What have you learned so far?"

Dove's frown deepens. What is he asking her to understand? The souls of the three reincarnated across multiple lifetimes, searching for the halved souls of the goddess. That much made sense. But only Iris had been a colorless, had been affected with something like the Drain.

She blanches. "Are—" she pauses, biting her lip, afraid to say what her thoughts now scream is correct. Something inside her stirs. "Are the colorless reincarnations of Iris?"

The librarian's face falls, but Dove senses it's not because she is wrong, but because she is right. The sadness that pours from him is palpable. He doesn't confirm if she is correct. Instead, he reaches forward and turns the next page in the book.

"Please, continue," he says.

Dove glances back down to a new title page—this time, it reads, *The Lux and the Umbra.*

Centuries later, after the disappearance of the Goddess and the splitting of her soul, the three searched for these broken pieces, hoping they may reappear in the people of the islands. After all, they'd reincarnated. It was their hope that in turn, the two halves of the Goddess' soul had also done the same.

One was easier to find than the other. A rare,

black-souled child was born two centuries after the Goddess disappeared. This was the piece of the Goddess that fell deep into the sea. Her soul sparkled like the depths of the ocean and swirled with the colors of the Goddess' tail.

They called this piece of the goddess the Umbra.

They searched for her other half, the piece that had ascended to the sky in a shaft of sunlight. But one such incarnation was never found.

Iris' incarnations, the colorless, the Solum Iris, were found often, across many generations. Born without a soul color at all and doomed to a life of solitude. But the three found that if a colorless did not know they were such, they could have relatively happy, normal childhoods.

The three established a school on the islands and held the mirror within. If they could wait until the reincarnations of Iris were older, they thought maybe it would be easier to spare them from their inevitable fate. However, this caused other issues. Ones that, if not remedied, could spell disaster for the islands and the Goddess' beloved children.

The only possible method the three could hope for to stop the cycle of destruction of the colorless was to reunite the halves of the Goddess' soul. But the light half, the Lux, was mysteriously missing for many generations.

The three's goal is to find the missing halves of

the Goddess' soul and reunite them. They do not know what may happen when they are brought back together once more, but their hope is that the cycle of reincarnation will end upon reuniting the halves.

"Am I the Umbra?" Rory's question cuts through Dove's focus.

The librarian bows his head. "Yes, Rory. You are the reincarnation of one half of the goddess' soul."

"Then where is the Lux?" she asks.

Something is burbling in Dove. A question, floating to the surface of an ocean full of light. She thought herself colorless—a reincarnation of the soul of Iris. But she does not cause the Drain and has not faded after realizing her soul color.

And this inexplicable pull she's always had toward Rory. Like Rory was something right, a missing piece of her that she's been searching for her entire life. Like now that they are together, she is whole.

The librarian watches Dove with a knowing look on his face. "I was not sure for some time, but after what I have witnessed today, well, I think you know the answer, Dove."

Rory turns her beautiful face to Dove, her eyes sparkling in the light from the setting sun. There's hope gleaming there, and something deeper. She wants to hold it close, whatever this little, fluttering thing in her heart is.

Dove nods, her eyes never leaving Rory's. "It's me. I'm the Lux, aren't I?"

18

REUNION

*D*ove sits on the edge of her bed. She's in her nightclothes, the loosely fitted fabric soft on her skin. It's cool in the room; it caresses her warm skin like a whisper.

She picks at a small snag in her pants. The window casts golden light across their room—it's only sundown, and Dove still is reeling from everything that has happened in the last day.

Jasper, gasping and losing his color at the entrance to the library, then miraculously healed him only hours later with Rory's help. Because of this incredible feat, the librarian, who is apparently a reincarnation of one of the original three, has concluded that she must be the missing half of the Goddess' split soul.

The fabric catches on her nail and tears a small opening on the knee. Dove twirls the loose thread around her finger, absent-mindedly doing her best to *not* think about how much her life has changed in such a small amount of time.

Unfortunately, that doesn't work.

It's too much to handle. All she has known about

herself and the world she inhabits is in disarray, her entire worldview rent apart and pieced together in a shape she doesn't recognize.

Too many questions remain—who is the reincarnation of Iris in this lifetime? Who has been causing the Drain? And the most important question of all...why have all the victims been so close to her?

Her neck spasms—she's been holding her shoulders as high as they will go, pinching them nearly to her ears. She tries to relax, rolling her head in circles and massaging the muscles in her jaw. It helps, but her body still screams in protest.

Dove has to admit to herself that she is simply exhausted. Such questions can wait until tomorrow. After all, she knows now that anyone else affected by the Drain can be cured with a touch from Rory and herself.

Rory. Her face pops into Dove's mind: the crooked smile, the wild hair, and her gut twists and turns. The attraction she's felt and the inexplicable pull make sense now. Rory is her other half, the person destined for her until the end. The gravity of it scares her, but not nearly as much as the thought of a life without Rory in it.

She can admit it. She loves Rory, and in more ways than one. She loves Rory like a flower loves the sun, or like a bee loves the cerise blooms. She loves her in a way that makes it impossible to imagine what life was like before loving her. She loves her like Rory was designed just for her. And in a way, she supposes she has been.

It settles over her, winding around her heart like a cat between her ankles. Soft and warm like the sun, and she opens her face toward it. She can settle into this. If nothing else makes sense, then loving Rory is the one thing that does. Dove has been incomplete until now.

It's true, she realizes. She needs Rory—a life without

her is a life incomplete, a life without sun or water or rain. A life without color.

The door opens; Rory has returned, bearing a bag full of something steaming. Dove is lost, the beast that purrs in her chest at the sight of Rory is impossible to ignore. Something must show on her face, because Rory sets the food on the desk and immediately rushes to Dove and squeezes her hands.

"What's wrong?" she asks, and Dove can't ignore the overwhelming urge to kiss the wrinkle between her brows.

But she can't move—she's frozen in place. She doesn't want to move for fear Rory will release her hands. But she wants to wrap herself around Rory, to bury her face in that wild mane of hair and lose herself in the warmth of her other half.

"I—" How does she explain this thing inside of her that is entirely too big to contain?

Rory watches her, those beautiful blue eyes wide with concern and something else Dove thinks might reflect this bursting inside of her chest. Rory is her other half, but she is also Rory's other half. Maybe...

Dove untangles her hand and lifts it tentatively to Rory's face, brushing a lock of hair from her cheek. Rory stays still. She tucks the lock behind Rory's ear and pulls her hand away, but before she can get far, Rory grabs it again.

"Dove...what are you doing?"

Her stomach lurches. Maybe she is alone. This was a mistake. Dove tries to pull away, but Rory only holds on tighter. Her eyes are burning, intense and roiling in the fading golden light.

Dove shakes her head and turns away. "I don't know. I don't know what this is, Rory. I'm—" She swallows the lump in her throat. "I'm scared of this, of us."

Rory's grip on her hands softens. "Oh, Dove."

The blush rises on Dove's cheeks. She got ahead of herself, let herself get too deep into what she was feeling and now she has strained the best relationship she's ever had. She doesn't know if she will ever recover from this, if *they* will recover.

"Dove, look at me," Rory says softly, releasing a hand to touch Dove's cheek. "You and I are two halves of a whole—isn't that incredible?"

Dove turns to face Rory and is met with that crooked smile she loves so much. "But do you feel the same things I do? It's...overwhelming."

She leans in, her face inches from Dove's, their lips aligned but not touching. "If this is overwhelming, let me drown."

Rory closes the gap, pressing her lips to Dove's softly at first. Dove melts into it. Her eyes close, her shoulders relax, and the world seems to align itself at the center where their lips meet. Their fates are intertwined and now their hearts are, too. The world is finally right, and Dove's heart is light.

Dove moves her hand to twine in Rory's hair, and Rory melts against her. Something in her pulls, no, *yanks* her deeper toward Rory. As if the very core of her soul is pulling from her chest and reaching.

She has always imagined her soul like a swirling ball in the center of her chest; she still imagines it so as Rory's lips pull away from hers. But now, as the other girl sits back on her heels, Dove imagines that ball of light slowly stretching, lengthening into a cord that has wrapped itself around the void that is Rory's soul. That instead of being two distinct beings, they have morphed and braided into one.

Fate, destiny, or chance. Whatever she wants to call

it, Dove knows this is exactly where she is meant to be.

Rory looks away, cheeks flushed. "I'm sorry if that was too sudden."

"It wasn't." Dove's voice is surprisingly steady compared to the torrent inside of her. "It was...nice."

Nice. That wasn't it at all—it was transcendent, ethereal, and a million other things Dove couldn't ever hope to put into words. But did Rory feel all these things too? How could she ask? How could she know if she didn't ask?

Rory just chuckles. Her smile is different than normal. The crookedness is still there, but there is a softness to its edges that Dove has never seen before. Something in it is peaceful, and although there is a storm of emotions inside of her, the sight of that smile is like a burst of sunlight through the clouds.

Dove watches, breath stuck in her throat, as Rory climbs gracefully off the bed and retreats to the desk where their food awaits. She gestures to the carpeted floor, eyes sparkling.

"Just like that time." She sits cross-legged on the floor and waves a fork at Dove. "Come on, the food's going to get cold if you keep gawking at me."

"You're just—"

Rory cocks an eyebrow. "Just what?"

Dove doesn't reply. She doesn't know. Rory is everything all at once. She keeps stopping herself, keeps tripping on her words. She doesn't know how to express what's inside of her, but she wants nothing more than for Rory to know. It's a sweet sort of pain, the irritation of being filled with all this love and having nowhere for it to go.

But as she settles next to Rory on the floor and gratefully accepts a fork, she realizes that maybe that's not entirely true. This is love—the simple gestures, the small things. Each time Rory stood by her side and made her feel seen. Every time Rory spent hours in the library, haunting the stacks for more information about the colorless or the Drain. When Rory would fetch food for her, or when she'd hold an umbrella in the rain.

Or when she gifted a piece of sea glass and told Dove it was just like her.

Love didn't need words; it was simply there. It always had been. She has just been too distracted to notice. But now that she's found it, she sees it in everything.

Dove pretends to be distracted by her food, but she knows Rory's watching her. She makes a noise through a mouthful, somewhere between confusion and a grunt.

Dove chuckles. "How long, Rory?"

Rory swallows, then stabs her fork into her food unceremoniously. "How long, what?"

"How long have you known you felt this way about me?"

Rory contemplates Dove, her blue eyes intense but full of mirth. "I wondered when you'd ask." She laughs to herself, a quiet thing, before continuing. "For a long time, now. But I knew you had your own life to deal with. Adding me into the mix was…too much."

Dove sets her fork down, too. "Well, it's not too much now."

Rory leans in, a smirk spreading across her lips, "Now we're just two halves of a whole, reunited. If anything, everything before this wasn't enough."

And there they are—the words Dove has been searching for this whole time. "Everything before wasn't enough," she echoes, nodding.

19

———

AZURA

Dove returns to the chancellor's office in the morning, Rory by her side. Any other arrangement would be wrong, now that their souls are reunited.

There are still too many unanswered questions, and she needs to figure them out before someone else falls victim to the Drain. Dove hopes that Chancellor Brigaine will know more or at least know where she must start.

"Dove." The chancellor's eyes shift. "And Rory." A glimmer of something Dove thinks is joy sparkles in her gaze.

Rory nods, holding her chin high in a stance that says *just try to kick me out.* But the Chancellor does no such thing. She smiles instead. The pleasure that radiates from her is familiar to Dove—in fact, it's like the librarian, Aurus, all over again.

The Chancellor gestures to the leather chairs that Dove is intimately familiar with and rounds her desk to sit. As Rory and Dove take their seats, she tents her long fingers on the desk and looks at them over her spectacles.

"I'm pleased you two are here. It seems Aurus did his job splendidly in informing you two of your origins, yes?"

Rory and Dove nod in unison. Dove speaks first. "Is it true, then? I'm the Lux?"

"And Rory is the Umbra, yes." She lets her hands fall to the desk. "We would like to confirm once more with the mirror, but after what you did for Jasper and Lapis, I cannot think we are wrong."

Dove glances around the spacious office, expecting to see the mirror already waiting, but she finds nothing other than the usual books and various scholarly items. The mirror is absent.

"Where is the mirror, then, Chancellor?"

She smiles. "It is on its way—along with Caerulum."

"Caerulum? The Healer?" Dove's heart flutters as she recalls what she learned from Aurus's massive tome. "Are all the reincarnations going to join us?"

The chancellor smiles wider, more mischievously, as if she knows something the girls do not. "I have summoned Aurus, yes. As for Lustro...well, I am here already so I suppose we are only missing Iris."

Rory's mouth drops agape. Dove wants to do the same. The remnants of the Goddess' soul inside her purr against the truth—she is indeed the reincarnation of the Scholar. But who exactly will be Caerulum? Is it someone she already knows, or someone brand new? Her heart is loud in her ears, but her chest fizzes, full of anticipation that bubbles like sea-foam.

The door squeaks, and on its threshold is the Aura Mirror, still covered by the sheet. A figure strides behind it, their long, dark blue cloak swishing behind them.

Hyacinth appears from behind the mirror, a wide grin stretching her dark painted lips. "Hi again, Dove, Rory."

Rory whips her head back around to the chancellor. "*Hyacinth* is Caerulum?" Her words come out slurred, stumbling over themselves in a rush to escape.

Hyacinth chuckles. "I see Aurus did his job." She sighs, then places her hands on her hips. "I am indeed Caerulum. It's lovely to see the two halves of our beautiful Goddess reunited once more."

A blush creeps up her cheeks. All she can do is bow her head, but Rory grabs her hand and holds it in the air like a trophy. "So much for not allowing Dove to have a partner, huh?"

Hyacinth laughs. "So much for that rule, indeed."

The chancellor stands from her chair and approaches the mirror and Hyacinth, planting a kiss on her cheek. "Thank you for bringing this out once again for me. I can't recall in all my years of being chancellor ever needing to bring the mirror out so many times."

"These are incredible times," Hyacinth says with a shrug.

She pulls the sheet from the mirror and positions it with a few gentle tugs. Her aura glows brilliant blue in the reflection as she adjusts, but there is something deeper, wilder, about it than other auras Dove has seen in the mirror. The swirling intensity of Hyacinth's color is hypnotizing. Was this the presence of Caerulum?

The chancellor gestures to Dove. "Come. Let's see the Lux in full glory."

Dove's heart speeds up; her palms prickle with sweat and the lump in her throat is hard to swallow. Because of course she is nervous. The last two times she has looked in this mirror, she has seen nothing but disappointment. What if, with this last look, she is exposed as a fraud? What if she isn't the Lux?

She steps before the mirror and both the chancellor and Hyacinth step out of frame. Dove watches her outline with rapt attention.

Seconds drag by until something appears. Something

faint but sparkling. It is the same slight waver of the surrounding air that she saw on the day of the Revelation Ceremony. The longer she looks, the more obvious it becomes.

The air is shimmering, like a still body of water that has been disturbed by a single drop of rain. It puckers and twists around invisible obstacles; a soap bubble in the afternoon sun, reflecting blues and reds, yellows and oranges, and every color she might name. The more she stares, the more she notices the subtle shades and differences in them.

She does not lack a color. She is all the colors in one.

Rory appears beside her, lips parted in awe. "It's beautiful, Dove."

But she isn't watching how her own aura pulls toward Dove's, how the colors in her deep, rich black entwine with the glimmers in Dove's. How they twist and wrap themselves around one another until they have combined into a resplendent, shimmering jewel. How their auras, despite belonging to two separate people, seem to bleed into one, as they were meant to be.

Their souls together look like the inside of the shells they find at the beach. Iridescent, with a thousand different colors and shades all mixed together in a cacophony of color.

She hears a soft intake of breath—Hyacinth. "It's... like nothing I've ever seen before."

"Incredible," the chancellor whispers at the same time.

Both of them sound reverent. Like they are praying to the Goddess whose soul they now see in front of them in the mirror. Dove thinks she understands. After all, the sight makes her want to drop to her knees.

The door to the chancellor's office opens and the

librarian appears; although he has come late, Dove can't help but feel he is right on time.

Aurus meets her eyes in the mirror, his wide-eyed gaze smoothing the wrinkles at the corners. His eyes fill with silver, tears yet unshed for a sight he has waited generations to see. A dream fulfilled.

"Azura," he whispers, voice thick with admiration. "My Goddess."

Dove returns her gaze to the mirror, to the spot where her soul has mixed with Rory's. Their combined auras make an iridescent rainbow, an explosion of color that makes her eyes swim. She once wished so fervently for a deep red, a ruby hue that would dance in the mirror like a jewel in the sun. She can almost see the old sheet she would hang behind herself as an homage to that wish. The pretend Aura Mirror that showed her a soul like her mother's.

But she doesn't wish for that, seeing the colors that burst before her eyes now. She could never have imagined a soul aura like this when she was little. It's more than she could have dreamed.

Rory is more than she could have wanted, too. She watches the other girl's eyes in the mirror, watching how they travel over the swirls and spots that Dove's gaze focused on just moments before. How they linger on the spot just above their hearts, where a shimmering, braided thread of red, yellow, and blue are the strongest.

This is their connection, their bond. The lasting vestiges of the Goddess inside of them both.

The chancellor comes behind them, her swirling golden aura pulling toward theirs. "I cannot stress how overjoyed I am that we have finally found both halves of the Goddess' soul. But—" She turns her eyes on Dove. The way her eyes crinkle in the corners reminds Dove of the wrinkle that would appear between her own mother's brows when she would deliver unpleasant news. "I fear we have wronged you, Dove. And for that, I am deeply sorry."

Whatever Dove expected the chancellor to say, it wasn't that. She holds up both her hands and shakes them. "How could you have known?"

"Our ignorance does not justify how you have been treated," the chancellor continues. "No matter what I say here, it will not fix the irreparable damage that has been done to your experience at Prism Academy."

Dove is left speechless, unsure how to respond to the chancellor's apologies. After all, an apology is not what she expected to receive today. But Dove is not angry—she has never been truly angry. She knows it was no one's fault. They simply acted the best way they knew how. She couldn't fault them for that.

"And we will do all we can to ensure we are making up for our mistakes from here on out." The chancellor's face finally relaxes as she finishes her piece, nodding at Dove in the mirror.

Dove, finding it hard to continue looking at the chancellor in the mirror, turns her eyes back to Rory. In the mirror, the blue of Rory's eyes seems even brighter than it is when she turns to face her in reality. But when she finds their cool ocean blue, Dove is pleased to discover that she was wrong.

Rory's eyes *are* brighter. And they're shining, too.

Hyacinth breaks the spell that has settled over the room. Her voice is grave. "As glad as I am with this discovery, our job is not over. We still don't know who Iris' reincarnation is."

Dove's stomach somersaults. Guilt tugs at the lining of her abdomen, returning the worries from before to the forefront of her mind. This isn't over—she cannot forget the way Jasper looked when Drained of his color. She cannot forget the way Lapis looked when he collapsed in the dining hall. She was too quick to forget their suffering.

Rory steps away from the mirror, the braided thread above their hearts fading as she leaves the boundaries of its magic. It's still there, Dove knows. They just can't see it any longer.

"Then where should we start?" Rory asks, voice as grim as Hyacinth's. "Until someone else falls victim, we don't know how to even find the colorless."

Hyacinth tilts her head toward the mirror. "We have this."

"Redo the Revelation Ceremony? For everyone?" Dove counters quietly. She doesn't want to overstep her bounds, doesn't want to cause a fuss. But whoever Iris' reincarnation is, they have already avoided detection once with the mirror. It wouldn't be impossible for them to do it again. "Wouldn't you have found them already if the mirror could detect them?"

The chancellor frowns. They have missed the Solum Iris until now—simply parading the entire school before the mirror again wouldn't yield any new results.

Aurus, who Dove had forgotten about, steps next to the chancellor, his withered hands clasped gently before him. The bowtie around his neck is a deep shade of burgundy, surely a small nod to the reincarnation living inside him. It crinkles under his chin as he nods to Dove.

"She is right. The mirror would not easily identify Iris, especially not if she knows it is coming. She has…ways of avoiding detection. After all, she has grown cunning in all her years of revival."

Hyacinth frowns. "What do you mean? We know she causes the Drain, but how does she avoid detection?"

Dove watches them. The frown on her lips almost

hurts, but she can't stop it. What is the point of the Drain, from Iris' perspective? What does she stand to gain by Draining others of their color?

"Well," Aurus continues, "Iris was the first victim of the Drain. But in every reincarnation, she comes back without her color. Isn't the conclusion obvious?"

"She is replacing her color," Dove says, finally understanding. "She avoids detection because she is stealing colors from others. She doesn't appear colorless in the mirror that way."

Aurus nods. "That's right. I believe that whenever Iris Drains someone, she takes on their color for a while. If she plans it right, she'll know to Drain someone before she would have to get in front of the mirror again."

Dove had hoped this wasn't the case, but with the librarian's hypothesis, the pieces fall into place. It's why she and Rory can heal those affected by the Drain. After all, the Goddess was the one who gave soul colors to begin with. When taken, only the Goddess can return them.

Rory huffs. "Then shouldn't we be able to find them anyway with the mirror? If their color differs from what it was at their Revelation Ceremony, we know it's them."

The chancellor shakes her head. "That's only if their latest victim, Jasper, was a different color than their assigned house."

She deflates, but Dove pats her shoulder. "It's a good idea, Rory."

"It certainly is," Hyacinth adds. "And it could prove useful, even if used in a slightly different application."

All eyes turn to Hyacinth, where she leans against one of the leather armchairs. She is the picture of pensiveness, her brows furrowed and one finger scratching her pointed chin. They wait in silence for her to continue.

When she finally does, her voice is softer than Dove

has ever heard it. It is as if she is unsure of herself, a quality Dove has never associated with the leader of the Aegis Order.

"We must appear to be doing something about this epidemic. There is no way to avoid Iris's suspicions completely." She nods, her next words more confident. "The Aegis Order will conduct interviews. With the mirror present. We will not warn them ahead of time that we are doing this with the mirror present."

Rory nods, but Dove hesitates. The chancellor lays a hand on Dove's shoulder. "Something wrong?"

Dove's frown deepens. "Won't the other students simply talk about what is said in their interviews? If Iris isn't one of the first to be interviewed, she may know before they take place to Drain someone."

Hyacinth smiles wryly. "That would serve our purpose, Dove. There are a few possibilities—either we discover her in our interviews by her colorless soul in the mirror or we find a student whose soul color does not match their house. If neither of these occur, we have a smaller subsection of students from which to choose as possible culprits. After all, Iris will have to Drain someone *before* her interview if she wants to hide."

Aurus nods. "It's not a foolproof plan, but it is certainly a start."

Hyacinth bobs her head in agreement. "We can tell students to keep quiet about their interviews as well. We *are* the Aegis Order, after all."

Rory grabs Dove's hand and gives it a reassuring squeeze. The plan, as Aurus said, isn't perfect. But it is a step in the right direction. Dove's insides are too tight, but a small rush of cool relief washes over her when Rory's hand grabs hers. Her skin is warm, not hot. Just enough to impress upon Dove that she's not alone.

"Alright," Dove agrees.

Rory's joy is immediate and loud. "Then, Chancellor, Hyacinth, what should we do?"

The chancellor shakes her head. "Absolutely nothing. You've done enough. We'll need you ready to heal in case another student falls ill to the Drain. Other than that, you must proceed as usual. Because the student body believes Dove to be colorless, we must continue to upkeep that facade. Hopefully, that will lure the real Iris into a false sense of security."

To serve as the decoy. Dove understands. She doesn't enjoy the small twinge of guilt. But the alternative, she reminds herself, is to do nothing. And Jasper's pale face twisted in pain is enough of a reminder that doing nothing is simply not an option.

Steeling her nerves, Dove squeezes Rory's hand back. "We're ready."

Hyacinth's smile is wild. "Then let's catch Iris."

20

———

IRIS

everal days pass as they solidify a plan to catch Iris. There are two things, Hyacinth says, that are the most important for Dove and Rory to remember.

First, they must not appear to know more than any other student. If they do, suspicions that they are involved could spell trouble for the school and for the Aegis Order.

And second, they must not reveal the fact that Dove is not colorless. Hyacinth and Aurus both believe that the real incarnation of Iris thinks themself safe thanks to Dove's very public Revelation Ceremony results.

But now that the plan is finalized, it's time to put it into action.

An assembly is called, and the entire student body of Prism Academy gathers in the Revelation Ceremony hall. Dove and Rory enter with the rest of the students, and Dove tries her best to appear as confused as the rest of the students murmuring around her.

That tickle in her chest that left her breathless during the Revelation Ceremony is gone; it's replaced by bone-deep dread.

And the question remains—who is Iris' reincarnation?

Chancellor Brigaine stands on the dais, her face placid. "Students of Prism Academy, we have gathered you today to address a serious issue on campus. While the specifics of this issue are sensitive, we are gathering you now to discuss our next steps."

The students sitting by Dove all mutter softly at the chancellor's words. The attack on Jasper was only days before, early enough that no one discovered he'd even been affected. Lapis, while significantly more public, had been a month and half earlier. Dove can't pick out the other students' exact words, but several themes arise in their whispered conversations.

Dove. The colorless. Lapis. The Drain.

But Dove steels herself—she is not the cause, but it doesn't ease the apprehension that perches on her shoulder and coos in her ear. Rory, seated beside her and so in tune with Dove's emotions, reaches a hand out to squeeze Dove's forearm.

The chancellor continues. "There have been a few instances of a disease on campus known as the Drain. While we believe we have the spread under control, we will interview students individually to assist the hospital in determining the source of the infection." She sighs, her face softening from fierce leader to imploring friend. "We are confident that the disease is handled; you are all very safe. That much we can guarantee."

The murmuring begins again with more fervor. They knew it would be a risk to announce it in such a public manner. But there is no other choice—word spreads too quickly on a campus such as this, and they need to be ahead of it, or at least somewhat in control of it.

The comforting squeeze of Rory's hand on her arm comes again. She hears the other students. She can imagine the weight of their stares settling in next to the perch of the dread on her shoulders.

She turns to face Rory, her lips curling into a soft smile. Rory watches her for a moment then returns a smile in kind. This is all Dove needs—the soft comfort of Rory beside her, and the overwhelming sense that with Rory, she is home.

The chancellor clears her throat, and the murmurs around them fade. "I know you have questions, but please save them for your meetings with the executive faculty. We will answer them as best we can during that time."

Dove watches as the chancellor nods, finishing her speech with a quick thank you and a dismissal of the students in the hall, promising their summons would be delivered to their residence halls sometime that same day.

Rory and Dove wait until the hall has cleared of most students before they take their leave. Dove's worry had calcified; she knows this is the best way to figure out who is Iris' reincarnation. But the pit in her belly is heavy. She worries for the other students and the danger they have exposed them to. She worries about Rory, about Roan, about Jasper and Lapis and every single person who has ever interacted with her.

She hasn't seen Roan since the morning Jasper fell ill and that worries her. He'd seemed fine that day as he'd left her in the library. But that worry in her stomach won't soften, no matter how hard she tries.

They leave the hall, hand in hand. Rory is uncharacteristically quiet but squeezes Dove's hand. The wind jostles Dove's hair and knocks something loose in her.

"I want to check on Roan," she says softly. "Do you want to come with?"

Rory nods immediately, no hesitation in her beautiful face. "Let's go."

At the Red dorm, there is an energy in the air. A fizzle that brushes over Dove's skin like a thousand tendrils of lightning. Rory must feel it too—her jaw is tense, the muscle clenching and unclenching as they approach the door.

Inside, the dorm is silent as death. No raucous laughter or flutters of conversation drift through the halls like usual. Dove's heels are too loud on the tile. A squeak from the heel of Rory's shoe sends an involuntary shiver through Dove's body. A door slams shut somewhere above.

It is as if the entire hall has reacted to their presence and has withdrawn. This is not what Dove expected when she came here for Roan. With the dorm like this, surely something terrible has happened?

Rory takes Dove's hand in hers, weaving their fingers together in the way Dove loves. Right now, Rory's fingers between hers are the only things keeping her heart from beating out of her chest.

Roan's room is on the second floor, three doors past the wide staircase. When they stop before his door, it is quiet. But as Dove raises her hand to knock, she hears a crash inside.

Rory shoves the door open with a heave of her shoulder and Dove flings herself through the open space. Her lungs are suddenly too tight, her chest shrinking in on itself as she scans the room.

But Roan stands in the center, unharmed. Before him lies a box, upturned, its contents scattering the floor. This must have been the source of the crash.

Rory stares at the items on the floor: a framed photograph with a crack in the glass, a seashell necklace, a now broken vial of sand, and a single piece of red ribbon tied in a bow. She doesn't recognize any of the items, but the photograph catches her eye. In it, two children sit upon a woman's lap, their smiles lopsided and brilliant.

She'd recognize that smile anywhere. It is Rory in the photo, young and happy. Beside her is a younger Roan, his eyes bright and clear. The woman looks so startlingly like her children that there is no doubt in Dove's mind this is their mother.

The one who fell ill just before Roan came to Prism. The one who eventually died from losing all her color.

The one who, just like Dove's mother, was a beautiful Red.

Her breath becomes shaky and shallow; the tightness in her chest grows as she stares at Roan. Realization settles over her, mixed with something much, much darker. Dove reaches a hand for Rory, pulling her back to stand beside her. Rory raises an eyebrow at Dove but obeys.

"Dove," Roan says, breathy and wild-eyed. "You see it now, don't you?"

Dove knows she is staring—knows her eyes are wider than they ever have been before. But she can't open her mouth. Her jaw is tight, her teeth creaking and groaning from the pressure.

Rory looks from Roan to Dove, her eyebrows knitted together. "See what?"

Roan doesn't respond, only stares more intently at Dove, waiting. For what, Dove isn't sure. He takes a single step forward, his shoes crunching over broken glass. The sound grates in Dove's ears, but she stands firm, her grip on Rory's hand tightening.

Rory tries again, her eyes fixed on her brother. "*See*

what, Roan?" Her voice is practically a growl now, low and ferocious in her throat.

Dove's jaw unlocks, and she gasps in a breath. "It's him, Rory. He's Iris."

It's as if the air in the room is sucked out through a vacuum at Dove's words, leaving everyone motionless. Roan waits, his mouth a thin line. Rory stares at her brother with a look that Dove has never seen her wear before. And Dove watches, waiting for Roan to confirm what she has said.

He frowns, the wrinkles beside his lips deep from frequent use. His expression is not one of pride or joy, but of pain.

"I thought—" His voice is weak. He lifts a hand to his chest, splaying his fingers over his heart. "I thought you were like me, Dove. You are colorless. Nothing. A soul devoid of the Goddess' gift."

Dove doesn't know what to say. She could object, tell him the truth of her soul.

Dove watches Roan transform. His shoulders curl in on themselves, his eyes drop to the floor, and he shrinks. This sunshine incarnate, this boy who has been nothing but kind and valiant to her suddenly becomes small.

"I never wanted to hurt anyone. I only wanted to help you, Dove."

"Why?" came the question Dove knew Rory must have been holding back. "Why did you do any of it then?" Her voice quavered, but she stayed firm, locking eyes with her brother.

Roan finally dropped his head, staring at the sand and broken glass beneath his foot. "I didn't know, at first. When I was ready to come to Prism, when Mom got sick, I didn't know. I thought I'd just inherited her color. But after she died, I started feeling sick too. I couldn't figure out how to get better, so I tried a little of everything. Then, finally, I discovered the cure for my sickness."

Rory's face is ashen. "It was…you. You killed Mom."

"I didn't mean to!" Roan cries, whipping his head up to look at Rory. Fat tears rolled down his cheeks. "I didn't know that prolonged contact was the trigger to Drain someone."

Dove takes Rory and pulls her behind her, getting between the siblings. She needs to understand. "So, what is the cure for your sickness?"

"The Drain," Roan says quietly. "I steal someone's color, and it heals me. But when they die, their color leaves me too."

Rory's warmth moves away from Dove's back and their hands unwind. She turns to see Rory has turned away completely, hands over her mouth and silent tears streaming down her face. Dove's own eyes swim at Rory's distress, but if Rory is like this now, then Dove must be her strength. After all, Rory has been her strength for so long, it is only fair Dove repays the favor.

"So, Lapis? Jasper?" Dove asks.

"Lapis was…the first time I did it on purpose. I thought…" He covers his face with his hands. "I thought I was helping you."

"Jasper?"

Roan lowers his hands. If she touched Roan's cheek now, would she feel the shame on her fingers like a cold sweat?

"I was…" He looks at the ceiling. "I don't know, jealous?"

Dove goes cold. While it's true that Lapis had been nasty to Dove, it doesn't excuse what Roan did. And for Jasper to have been a victim too, for no better reason than simple jealousy?

Guilt wells in her chest, that ever-present sense that she is to blame for the awful things that have happened. But she fights back against that rise, that burning in her chest.

"Why would you think I'd be okay with hurting someone else?"

He lifts his head. "Because you're like me, aren't you? Don't you have to do this too? Steal colors to keep yourself alive?"

"No!" Rory's voice is raw, ragged and sanded down like she's been screaming for hours. "Dove isn't like you. She would never hurt others to save herself."

She's never been given the chance, Dove thinks. Until now, she's kept her distance from everyone, never learned how to rely on anyone but herself. It doesn't change the fact that Rory is right.

But Dove understands Roan, just a little. She faces Rory, the other half of her soul. "Maybe we can heal him. Like we did to the others."

Rory's face is flushed, red-cheeked and splotchy. Her hands tremble as Dove takes and squeezes them. In that touch, Dove can feel her pain. The betrayal of a brother she loves, the re-opening of the pain her mother's death caused. And beneath it all is a small, tiny flicker of hope. A white-hot flame that burns beneath all the others.

She nods, a brief bobbing of her head that if Dove wasn't watching her with a fixed, intense gaze, she might have missed. She knows Rory must be struggling with all that has come to light, but this is Dove's only idea. Her only chance to fix what has been broken for so long.

Roan looks between them, confusion written on the lines in his face. He looks so much older now, with the weight of what he's done in the open. "What do you mean, heal me? Like you did to who?"

"Jasper and Lapis," Dove says. "We are something very special, Roan, and I think together we might heal you."

Roan still looks perplexed. Dove simply reaches for him, toward his hand. Realizing what she is about to do, Roan jerks his hand away.

"No!" he cries, cradling his hand to his chest. "You can't! If you aren't like me, Dove, I will Drain you of your color. I don't want to do that to you."

Dove considers him. He never wanted any of this—that much is obvious. There is more to Roan's story yet, and Dove wants to make sure he can tell it. Without this, he will never have the chance.

"Please. We'll be different."

"You can't know that." He turns his head away from her, too.

Dove is at a loss. She knows if she doesn't try to help him now, she may never again have the chance. When all this is over, she doesn't know what will happen to Roan. But she can't live with herself if she doesn't do everything she can.

She reaches forward and grabs one of Roan's hands. At the same moment, Rory does the same. Their actions are so in sync, one would think they had planned it.

Roan doesn't struggle. He just stares, wide-eyed, at Dove and Rory while they close their eyes and begin praying to the Goddess that lives inside of them.

21

———

DESTINY

*T*his is not like last time, Dove thinks as a scene forms behind her eyes.

Around her, a wide plain stretches. The sky is a dusky purple, akin to her namesake. The ground reflects the sky in a way she's never seen before. It is as if she is standing in a puddle the size of an ocean. It's shallow enough that she does not sink into the water.

She moves her foot; a single ripple echoes across the still water, breaking the monotonous plain of purple before her. She looks down to her feet and gasps.

Dove is made of starlight. She is transparent but still holds her shape. She lifts her hand, mixing her blue transparent skin with the purple sky. Around her, whorls of gold and blue and red dance in an invisible wind. It reminds her of the way her soul looked in the Aura Mirror, and she smiles for the beauty of it.

"Azura?" A voice echoes across the plain. Dove does not see where it comes from, nor does she see anyone appear on the plain when she turns. But that name, it echoes in her soul. It feels right and good, like coming home or eating a sweet roll. Like she's been waiting her whole life to be called by that name.

Shadows swirl, mixing with a thick and heavy mist that obscures the sky from her vision. The expanse turns foggy, and she cannot see, not even when she waves a hand in front of her face.

She takes a single step forward, the thin layer of water trickling between her bare toes as she does. Then another step, and another. The water parts for her as she walks, rising around her and coating her transparent skin in droplets that look like diamonds. The fog is thick but not oppressive. She walks through it easily, relishing the way it caresses her skin, hair, and face.

And when she appears on the other side, a figure waits for her.

She is small, sitting on the ground cross-legged with her eyes closed. It is as if she is meditating, or possibly asleep. But when Dove emerges from the fog, she opens her eyes. They are a brilliant shade of blue, reminiscent of the eyes Dove has stared into so many times since coming to Prism. They're like Rory's eyes.

Her full lips part in a smile, and her long, white hair ruffles in the same invisible wind that swirls the colors around Dove. She wears a simple white dress that pools around her crossed legs.

In her lap rests a book.

Dove recognizes it—it's the one the librarian had locked away behind his desk. The one that tells the story of the islands, of the Goddess, and of Iris.

As soon as she thinks of the first child born of the Azura isles, the girl before her smiles. "Hello." It is the same voice that called earlier, that same sweet melodic tone that gave Dove peace.

"Hello." The voice that emerges is not her own. "It is good to see you, Iris."

"Likewise, Azura. Are you here to help me?"

Dove nods, feeling as if her body is wholly not her own. She is not in control—maybe she never was. Not since coming here. She was the Goddess' vessel now, the vehicle through which her soul would give Iris peace.

Iris smiles again as she stares up at Dove. Her hands rest loosely on top of the book. She is not possessive of it, nor does she seem attached to it. It is simply there, resting, waiting for someone else to come take it.

Dove reaches forward and takes the book from Iris' lap. She doesn't protest or stop Dove. She simply watches with curious eyes as Dove steps back, book in her hands.

Iris nods. "I see. This is the end, isn't it?"

Dove watches Iris with a discerning eye. The other girl glows from within, as if her skin overlays a skeleton made of gold. The magic within Iris is palpable. Dove can practically smell it—fresh cut grass and stardust. Lillies and bonfires. Spun sugar and spring water. It changes with each breath, as if the magic is shifting itself to be pleasant and palatable. As if it is waiting, *begging*, to be noticed.

She thinks she understands now why Iris was so impatient. To be granted such a gift and ignore its pleas is difficult to imagine even for the Goddess herself.

Something inside Dove unfurls. There, beneath it all. It rests beneath her love for Rory, beneath her determination to save Roan, beneath her desire to know herself. It is buried beneath the shame of disappointing her parents, beneath the weight of responsibility she placed upon herself.

It unfurls, and Dove sees it for what it is. This stone of guilt that has been here all this time. But the guilt is not hers—it never has been. It is the Goddess' guilt. *Azura's* guilt.

But watching as Iris twirls a tendril of Dove's aura around her finger, the knot of guilt dissolves. It spirals from her like a leaf upon a river, rushing away from her. It sparkles as it leaves, twirling up into the lavender sky and disappearing into the ether.

At its departure, Dove is light. Iris watches her, face impassive. The smile is gone, but so is the tendril of Dove's aura.

Iris sighs, a lovely thing filled with the weight of centuries. "I'm so tired, Azura."

"I know." Dove reaches forward to lay a hand on Iris' brow. "Be at peace."

Iris closes her beautiful stormy ocean eyes.

The plain dissolves. The water beneath Dove's feet is sucked away, the lilac sky disintegrates into darkness.

When Dove opens her eyes again, she is back in Roan's room, holding his and Rory's hands, and sunlight streams through the open window. Dust motes swirl in its rays, hovering over Roan's head like the tendrils of her aura Iris played with in the vision.

His eyes are closed, so much like the last vision of Iris. He holds Dove's hand tightly, squeezing it like it has anchored him to this life. And maybe it has. Dove wants to wake him, wants to know if Iris' soul is truly at rest. But she is afraid to pull him from the land of dreams too quickly.

Rory does not hesitate. She lets go of Dove's hand and rests it on her brother's cheek, patting it gently. "Roan?" she says. "Did it work?"

His eyes flutter open gently, as if he is waking from a dream. His lashes drip with tears, running down his cheeks in rivulets. But when he opens his eyes, they are no longer the stormy cerulean that she remembers. They have turned to honey, golden brown in the sunlight. A testament to Iris' disappearance from his body.

His eyes meet Dove's and confusion sweeps across his features. "What just—"

"Your eyes!" Rory cuts him off with a shriek. "Why are they brown?"

Roan lifts a hand to touch his cheek, opposite of where Rory still held his face in her hand. She lets go of Roan's hand to grab both sides of his face and turn him to face her. Dove doesn't know what Rory is looking for in Roan's face, but when Rory nods, she figures she must have found it.

Roan gently pries Rory's hands from his cheeks but doesn't let them go. "I feel…" He trails off. Dove watches with bated breath. But Roan stays silent, not meeting either of their gazes. Instead, he stares at the floor, brows knitted together.

Rory huffs. "Feel what, Roan? Are you okay?"

His brows stay firmly scrunched together as he replies slowly. "I feel…empty."

Dove's muscles relax—she hadn't realized she was so tense. But she thinks she understands. Roan has been inhabited by Iris for so long that it is strange indeed to lose her so suddenly.

She wraps Roan in a hug, Rory following her lead without hesitation. His hands, now untangled from Rory's, don't move from his lap. But he leans his head on her shoulder and his shoulders drop.

They don't move for some time. The three of them stay wrapped up in their embrace, leaning into each other as if the desire to meld as one has taken all of them over. Roan eventually wraps his arms around both Rory and Dove, fisting the backs of their uniforms in his hands.

She knows this may be the last time they can hold him like this—he has to answer for what he's done. But Dove doesn't care right now. All she wants is to melt into the siblings and soak in their warmth.

"Dove, Rory." Roan's voice is a knife's edge—sharp but so thin. "I'm sorry. I'm so sorry."

She squeezes him tighter in response. Rory buries her head in his shoulder.

Rory is the first to respond. "I forgive you, Roan."

Dove knows that forgiveness isn't given easily—that trust must be re-earned. But for the Goddess that purrs in her heart, forgiveness is the only option. It is the answer, and the answer she wants to give.

"I do too," she whispers into his hair. His shoulders drop.

And when they finally break, Roan's brown eyes are filled with determination and hope. The same hope that Dove sees in Rory's eyes and in her own when she stares into the mirror.

Three students dressed in vibrant yellow uniforms are leaving as Dove, Rory, and Roan arrive at the chancellor's office. This image of the solid wooden door before her will be burned into the back of her eyelids forever for how often she has stood before it. But something about this time feels final.

When Dove and Rory enter, Hyacinth turns from where she stands before the chancellor's desk. Her eyebrows raise in surprise, then knit together when her eyes find Roan behind them.

"Has something happened?"

They both turn in unison to face Roan, who nods

and approaches Hyacinth. His back is straight as he approaches, every line in his body taut with anticipation. He knows this is the end, and that is okay.

"Please forgive me." Roan's voice is tight. "But I fear I'm the one you've been looking for."

Hyacinth's face softens into surprise, a silent parting of her lips. Her eyes bounce between Dove and Rory, but she says nothing. In the corner, the Aura Mirror stands lonely and tall. Hyacinth glances at it, then back to Roan. He's still, head bowed, and hands clasped in front of him.

She shakes her head as if to ward off a tickle, then gestures for Roan to approach the mirror. "Let's have a look at you, then."

He nods and approaches the mirror. His head stays bowed, as if he is afraid to look at himself in the mirror. But when he stands before it, something glimmers around him. It is deep and dark, but rich. A thousand shades all tied up into one beautiful swirling dance around Roan's head.

Dove stares, stunned, at Roan's beautiful hue. "Roan," she whispers, tone reverent. "You're…"

Hyacinth stares too, but her face is soft, like she is witnessing a pleasant memory. Before Iris lost her color, she too was a deep, beautiful blue like the color that now shines around Roan's outline in the mirror.

"Iris," Hyacinth whispers. But she glances down at Roan, still dressed in his Red house uniform. It is wrong, and Hyacinth glances back at Dove and Rory, confusion written on her face.

Rory is speechless, struck mute by the color of her brother's true soul color in the mirror, so Dove explains for Hyacinth.

"We released Iris," she says. "Like how we cured Jasper and Lapis."

Hyacinth slides her gaze to Roan once more. "So, he hasn't stolen another color?"

Dove shakes her head.

"Then this is…"

Roan smiles, his face brilliant. "This is my true color, isn't it?"

Rory flings herself at him, wrapping her arms around his shoulders and burying her face in his neck. He returns her gesture, his arms snaking around his sister and squeezing. Something inside of Dove settles, like sand washed onto shore and left to dry pleasantly in the sun. The overwhelming feeling of rightness takes root inside her chest. Like this is what she has been waiting for all this time. The world to right itself, and the cycle to be broken.

That thought passes through Dove like a cold knife—if Iris is gone, what will happen to the Three?

"Hyacinth," Dove says, meeting the woman's violet eyes. "What will happen to Caerulum, Lustro, and Aurus? What about the Goddess?"

Hyacinth does not react the way Dove expects. She waits for Hyacinth to have the same bone-deep dread as her, for her face to drop in fear and sweat to shine on her brow. But she does not react this way. Instead, Hyacinth closes her eyes and smiles.

"Don't you see?" The tone of her voice is reverent, like she's wrapping herself in a prayer. "We're free. Your presence means the end of this curse, the end of this cycle we couldn't break for generations. You, the missing piece, the other half of our Goddess' soul, is the last thing we needed for eternity to end. And now that you've released Iris, you can release us all."

A hand touches hers—Rory. She has returned to Dove's side and is smiling. "It's destiny, Dove, don't you think?"

Dove has never grasped the depth of destiny—but now, as she watches Roan's shimmering aura in the mirror, Hyacinth's gentle smile, and the way Rory's fingers weave with her own, she thinks maybe she understands.

22

———

BEGINNING

A full year passes in the wake of Iris' release. Roan is made to pay for his crimes by working for the Aegis Order, under the watchful eye of Hyacinth. Jasper and Lapis return to their classes with their color restored. Everything is in its place, and all is right with the world.

Especially for Dove.

Rory is by her side. Their affection has only deepened, their soul-deep bond carving a rune inside of their hearts that mirror each other's. The proclamation at the beginning of her enrollment at Prism is rescinded—Hyacinth quickly acknowledged that keeping the Goddess' soul separated would be cruel and unreasonable.

And their final task as the reincarnated Goddess is to release the souls of Caerulum, Lustro, and Aurus.

Today, it is Aurus's turn. The chancellor went first only a few days after Iris's release, and Hyacinth the month after. But the librarian held on to the Steward for longer. Aurus has been a part of him for so long, he said letting him go was a bigger challenge than he'd realized.

Dove sits beside Rory in the chancellor's office, the book of *Azura* resting on her lap. There's a bond with this book, an odd sort of affinity she didn't know one could have for an inanimate object. But it's there, anyway, resting in her chest like a contented cat in a puddle of sunlight. Warm and affectionate.

The door opens and Aurus steps into the office, wearing a burgundy bowtie. Dove smiles, unable to stop herself from recognizing the one her soul has known the longest in him. His aura sparkles when he passes the Aura Mirror, the perfect crimson Dove once wished for.

He sits across from Dove and Rory. The wrinkles around his eyes are deep as the curve of his lips grows.

Dove searches his face for any hint of apprehension or fear. She is met with an expression she cannot quite place. The twinkle in Aurus' eyes reminds her of the very first day she met him and of the day he showed her the book now resting in her lap. It is the twinkle of knowing something, a secret, that is soon to be shared.

He nods once and holds his hands out to Dove and Rory. They gracefully lay their hands in his, closing their eyes. His gnarled fingers wrap around hers.

Dove is used to the scene when their souls entwine by now. The vast expanse of nothing, the reflection of the lavender sky in the thin sheet of water at her feet. But something about this one is different.

The sun hangs lower in the vast empty sky than it ever has before. The once gentle breeze that blew up the hairs on the back of her neck is gone. The air isn't stagnant though—it's as if the world is holding its breath.

Before her stands a brilliant man with glowing golden hair. In this light, the combination of the lavender sky and his hair gives it an almost halo-like glow. He is clad simply in a cotton robe of rough fibers, his feet bare and setting the water around his feet to rippling as he rocks back and forth.

And when he turns, Dove looks into the eyes of the librarian in a face that is not the kind man she knows.

Instead, the man before her, Aurus, looks grim. His mouth is tight, the lines around his eyes deep. He holds himself ramrod straight, as if waiting for orders, not freedom. The surrounding energy is a stark contrast to the soft nature of this soul-place.

But when her eyes meet his, everything softens. The glow around his hair brightens, his hands relax, and the creases by his mouth turn from frown lines to smile lines. His eyes radiate peace. And Dove knows now that he has been waiting so long for this, for her.

He holds out a hand, smooth from calluses except for one by his middle finger—a writer's callus, she notes. Because Aurus, although a large man in his soul, was not a soldier, but a scholar. A steward of the Goddess' stories and her creations, the man trusted with the care of the world when she was gone.

And now that she has returned, now that her soul is here, he is set free.

Dove reaches forward to take the offered hand, a feeling rising in her chest that is too large to contain. She knows by now that it isn't hers, but Azura's. Even so, it threatens to burst from her chest as Aurus' hand closes.

"Azura." He says the Goddess' name, *her* name, with such tenderness. It is love there, embraced with reverence and pride. As if there is no one and nothing more important than her in his world. "You're here."

Dove nods. "I am. It's time, Aurus."

"I know," he says, smiling. "But may I have just one more moment with you? It has been so long since I've heard your voice."

"And so long since I've enjoyed yours," she replies. "How about you tell me one last story, Aurus?"

218

His smile is broad and brilliant, the color of the white-capped waves on the sea. He bows his head. "I believe I can do that, my lady."

The prickle starts behind her eyes, but the tears don't come. Aurus was the first, and now he will be the last of her children. Joy and sorrow entwine in her chest as Aurus clears his throat and begins his last tale.

"Long ago," he begins. His voice is full of mirth and Dove can't stop the smile that spreads across her own face in response. "When the Goddess plucked a red feather from her tail and created her Steward, she kissed the feather before setting it upon the sky. The mark she left behind formed the Steward's heart. Without her touch, the Steward never could have lived as he did."

Aurus tugs at Dove's hand, taking several small, tentative steps toward the vague horizon. She follows, and although she knows this story, she can't take her attention away from the man beside her.

"And many years later, when the Goddess died, the Steward was determined to wait for her until she appeared again. He lived hundreds of lives; his second life was that of a humble fisherman. Each fish he'd bring home would remind him of the way the Goddess had created the oceans and the life within."

Each step they take sends ripples out, their journey seemingly endless. But Dove knew they are only eternal because she wills it.

Aurus continues, his eyes on the horizon. "His other lives led him down many paths. He was a secretary, a mother, a traveler, a farmer, and a teacher. But in one life, he was a librarian. Ever since, he desired to continue this life of knowledge he'd found. It was his way of staying connected to the Goddess he'd lost, his way of keeping her memory alive."

His gaze rests on the horizon, where the sun hangs too low in the sky. His arm, still escorting her, slackens a fraction. When Dove glances down, her lips part in surprise. Aurus is fading.

"He chronicled her stories, compiling all of them in a single book he could use to keep her memories alive. He wrote each story he'd told the Goddess, every piece of information he could remember through his variety of lives. He hoped that by keeping her memory alive in between the pages of a book, she would reappear someday."

Aurus is fading quickly. Dove can see the hazy skyline through his body. His grip on her arm is even looser now, his incorporeal form having difficulty interacting with her solid one.

The end is nearing. It is soft, like a gentle wave on the beach. It ebbs ever closer, the gentle creep of the approaching finality caressing over her soul. It is not sad, she thinks as she turns her gaze to Aurus' face.

He is finally looking at her, his eyes the last things that still appear solid as his edges fade like fraying fabric.

"The end is not so terrifying. The end is only a new beginning. Now that the Steward's Goddess has returned, he can finally move on to the next great adventure. Although the end is a mellow cry, he will not shed any tears. Bittersweet as it may be, the Steward has reached eternal rest gazing upon the face of the Goddess he so dearly loved."

Dove's throat goes dry. She cannot feel Aurus' arm on hers anymore. It has dissipated into a sparkling mist, one that reminds her of the color of the Goddess' soul in the Aura Mirror. But the red of Aurus' soul is vibrant and deep, the last remnants of his beauty sparkling against the ripples that echo from Dove's feet.

"Aurus," she says, and her voice, just like before, is

not her own. "You live inside us all, in the drop of magic that shines in every one of my children. Thank you will never be enough, but it must be."

Aurus watches Dove as the last of his body fades, his eyes closing and disappearing into the red glitter that drifts into the horizon.

And when Dove opens her eyes, she is hollow. It seems that as Aurus disappeared, so too did the Goddess. The pit inside her chest is hollow and echoing, but she does not feel incomplete. Instead, she is light. A burden has been lifted from her shoulders.

It seems to Dove that releasing Aurus to the cosmos was the final tether holding the Goddess to Dove's soul. But if she is gone, what color remains?

The Aura Mirror still rests in the corner of the chancellor's office, its sheet pooled on the floor. Dove's gaze finds it, but is quickly interrupted by Rory's soft gasp and a small chuckle from the librarian.

"It seems," he says, "that I am turned loose."

Rory, on the other hand, is resting a hand on her chest. She looks to Dove, her eyes wide. "She's...gone?"

Dove nods. "She's gone."

Rory frowns. "I didn't know she would leave, too."

Dove didn't either. But whatever Dove is feeling now with the loss of the Goddess' soul inside her own, it isn't sadness or loss. Does Rory feel this, too?

Dove stands, eyes fixed on the Aura Mirror in the corner. She needs to know. With the Goddess gone, does she regain a color? Or will she stay the spectrum of colors the Goddess gave her? This is the only thing she fears. Not the absence of the Goddess or the hollowness in her chest.

Her reflection stares back, the soft violet of her eyes swirling in the afternoon light.

Rory comes to stand beside her, twisting their fingers

together and meeting Dove's gaze in the mirror. Her touch says, whatever happens next, we do it together. Dove squeezes her hand in gratitude.

In the mirror, her aura shines like it did before. Rory's twists, their intermixed soul colors iridescent and shining in the sun. They are all the colors. The Goddess left them this much, entrusting Dove and Rory with the last vestiges of her soul.

Dove squeezes Rory's hand one more time, their tangled souls going blurry as tears she's held back all this time finally spring to her eyes.

Whatever is next, they will do it together.

ACKNOWLEDGEMENTS

I find this set of acknowledgements particularly difficult to write. I started writing this little novel back in 2022, as a respite between my other, heavier stories. And it proved to be such a release of joy.

But nearing the end of the journey of completing Solum Iris, my mother-in-law, Cathy, passed away from a ten-month long battle with adrenal cancer. Cathy was the kindest, most loving soul this world has ever been graced with, and her loss is like snuffing out the sun. I want to acknowledge her role in my journey as an author, and how her love, kindness, and compassion shaped me into who I am today.

Because of her unyielding support and fervor for my passions, the doubts that inevitably surfaced while publishing a piece of fiction were easily quelled. Her unbridled joy to read my words and so many of my friends' words was a driving force in my pursuit of writing. She was the sun after days of rain, summer after a long winter, and there will never be another soul quite like her.

So in these acknowledgements, I want to thank her first and foremost for being an incredible cheerleader, friend, supporter, teammate, and mom. You truly were the best of us, Cathy.

As for the swaths of people who are still here, I want to appreciate them, too.

First, my husband, Ryan, who through all of this remained a bastion of strength and love. Without you, bee, I would never be able to accomplish any of this.

Your everlasting love and kindness, learned from your wonderful mother, will never cease to be my favorite thing about you.

Those who worked with me on this story–Lindsay, Brit, and Olivia, y'all made this beautiful thing come to life. This book wouldn't have become what it is without you, your ideas, your encouragement, and your talents. I am always lucky to find such incredible partners for each book I write, but this one was exceptional. Thank you, over and over, for all your work and participation.

To Judith–I've thanked you in every book I've written so far, and that won't change. You have proven, time and again, that distance does not diminish the quality of friendship. You may be entire oceans away from me, but your friendship and joy are permanently etched into my heart. Thank you for being such a wonderful friend and excellent alpha reader.

Paulina, Gina, Rachel, and Heather–I wouldn't be able to do any of this without you. You are exceptional friends, fantastic cheerleaders, and some of the most wonderful people I have ever had the blessing to meet, know, and love. You make this solitary ride of authoring not lonely at all, and most importantly, you make it fun.

And to each and every one of you who picked up this cozy little sapphic fantasy, I am indebted to you. You've once again made these dreams of mine come true. Without you, I wouldn't be an author. Without you, none of this would be possible.

ABOUT THE AUTHOR

T.M. Ledvina is an avid reader and writer with a bachelor of the arts in English, and loves all things fantasy and romance. They live in Madison, Wisconsin with her husband, Ryan, and certified good boy, Cori. When they aren't writing, you can find her watching anime, playing ttrpgs, or enjoying video games. Ledvina is the author of the Brimstone and Fire series.

tmledvina.com
On Instagram: @tiamae.books
Photo by Audrey Rice

www.ingramcontent.com/pod-product-compliance
Lightning Source LLC
Chambersburg PA
CBHW032252310726
48973CB00008B/2391